How to SURVIVE as a *teen*

How to SURVIVE as a
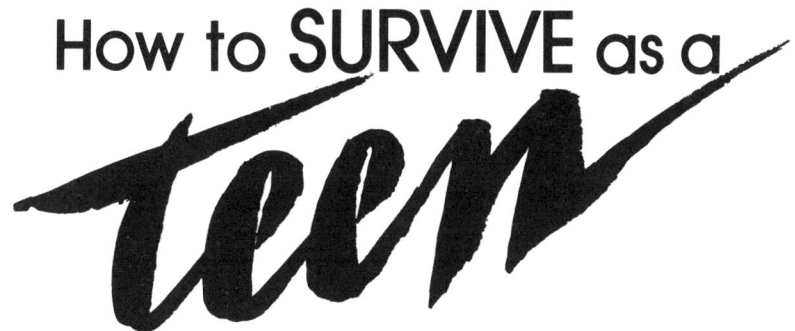

When No One Understands

Stevan E. Atanasoff

HERALD PRESS
Scottdale, Pennsylvania
Waterloo, Ontario

Library of Congress Cataloging-in-Publication Data

Atanasoff, Stevan E., 1959-
   How to survive as a teen : when no one understands / Stevan E. Atanasoff.
     p. cm.
   Summary: Offers guidelines for teenagers on ways of coping with a variety of problems involving self-esteem, friendship, sexuality, romance, parents, drugs, alcohol, and suicide.
   ISBN 0-8361-3478-8 :
   1. Teenagers—United States—Life skills guides—Juvenile literature. 2. Teenagers—United States—Conduct of life—Juvenile literature. [1. Conduct of life.]
I. Title.
HQ796.A757 1989   88-21285
305.2'35—dc19   CIP
                                                                         AC

HOW TO SURVIVE AS A TEEN
Copyright © 1989 by Stevan E. Atanasoff. Published by
   Herald Press, Scottdale, Pa. 15683; released
   simultaneously in Canada by Herald Press,
   Waterloo, Ont. N2L 6H7. All rights reserved.
Previous edition published by the author under the title,
   The Second Wind: Practical Help for Teenage Problems.
Library of Congress Catalog Card Number: 88-21285
International Standard Book Number: 0-8361-3478-8
Printed in the United States of America
Designed by Gwen M. Stamm
Cover photo by Allen Blosser

95 94 93 92 91 90 10 9 8 7 6 5 4 3 2

This book is dedicated to my little son,
ANDREW THOMAS.
My prayer is that you
and others like you
may grow to be happy, healthy,
and filled with genuine love for yourself,
all people everywhere,
and our God.

With Appreciation

No book is ever the product of one person. This one is no exception. I am deeply grateful and personally indebted to many fine people for all the help they have given to produce this book.

I extend my sincere thanks to the young people of my parish and our youth group who helped with interviews, research, suggestions, and criticisms; to my editors Professor Julian Shuchter and his very special wife, Jean, for their many hours of labor; to Don Hazle for his work with the computer; to Barbara Woolley for proofreading and suggestions; and to Paul M. Schrock and the staff of Herald Press for their fine work.

Most of all, I wish to thank my wife, Karen, for her typing and retyping the manuscript. Without her patience and support, this book could not have been written. God bless you all.

Contents

To My Young Friends 9
(Introduction)

1. I Guess I Don't Amount to Much............... 13
   (Self-Esteem)

2. Mirror, Mirror on the Wall,
   Who Is the Ugliest of Them All? 21
   (Looks)

3. They Can Make or Break You 29
   (Friendship)

4. Just Someone to Call My Own 39
   (Romance)

5. How Far Did You Go? 51
   (Teen Sexuality)

6. Oh My God, Not Me!..........................62
   (Teen Pregnancy)

7. There's No Place Like Home? 76
   (Parents)

8. Nasty Secrets................................93
   (Sexual Abuse)

9. It Didn't Start Out This Way! 103
   (Drugs and Alcohol)

10. No Way Out 117
    (Teen Suicide)

Some Closing Thoughts.........................130
(Conclusion)

A Letter from the Author........................134

About the Author 136

To My Young Friends

Most of you reading this have never met me and probably never will. You may even resent my having the nerve to call you friend when I know nothing about you personally. How can I, a complete stranger, know anything about your likes and dislikes, your struggles and pains, your needs, or your hopes and dreams?

You see, not long ago I was just where some of you are now. Those memories of my teenage years are quite fresh, and even if I could forget them, I wouldn't want to. Because I do remember those painful years, I have written this book. It is written for you. It is written for anyone who has ever had to struggle or felt like a nobody. It is written for you who feel depressed or lonely. It is written for you who are in real trouble and just don't know where to turn. It is written for you who carry deep pain inside because there seems to be no one who understands or cares enough to listen. It is written for you who feel like you've reached the end of the line and are about to "pack it in." Somewhere on these pages you will find words addressed to you.

This book deals with some of the real and difficult problems teenagers face today. It is based on my daily contact with young men and women much like you, on my own personal experiences, and on much reading and thinking. While the problems dealt with in this book are by no means the only ones you face, I am confident you will find much with which you can identify.

But this is not just a book describing problems. You know enough about them from your own experiences. The real purpose of this book is to help you face your problems and beat them, to help you know you have what it takes to lead a full and happy life.

The principles found in this book have been tried and tested by many. They are true and will work for you as they have worked for others. While they will not take away all your problems, they will put you firmly on the road to genuine happiness and success. But the book can't help you while it gathers dust on a shelf. Put the effort in and it won't let you down.

By the time you finish this book, I hope we will be friends. I hope you will come to believe in yourself and be your own best friend. If this book helps you through some dark times, writing it will be worthwhile.

This book is designed to be used. I know many of you hate to read, but read it anyway. Underline the parts you want to remember. Write in it. Carry it around with you. Turn to it as you would a trusted friend whenever you need a word of encouragement or reassurance.

Now set aside some time and let's get started. Life is too short to be unhappy, so make the effort to walk a better road. This book is your signpost. Remember, I'll be with you all the way.

Your brother on the road,
Steve

How to SURVIVE as a *teen*

1

I Guess I Don't Amount to Much

I want to ask you something. Think hard now and be honest. How do you really feel about yourself? When you go off to school each day (if you still go), do you like being there among friends or do you feel like a misfit? Do you enjoy your own company or do you find yourself boring? Can you stand on your own or do you need the constant approval of others? Do you believe that other people are better than you are?

If you didn't do too well on the questions, don't get too uptight about it. If you feel like a misfit today, or if you think everyone is so much better than you that you can't stand it, don't worry. We can work on this and changes can be made. Trust me and you will see for yourself.

When I was in high school, I was one of those guys

who was just there. I was not a bad kid. I was not very good either. I just floated through and I don't think either my fellow students or teachers would have noticed if I had dropped out for good.

I had a few friends, but for the most part I was afraid of people and felt inferior to them. I was afraid of girls and always felt that the other guys were stronger and far better looking than me. Feeling so inferior all the time, I tended to blend into the woodwork, hoping no one would see how much of a zero I really was.

The few times I had to come forward and emerge from my little shell were always awful and I dreaded them before, during, and after they happened.

I remember in Spanish class, we had to get up in front of our classmates and tell in the Spanish language what we had done over our vacations. How I hated that!

As I sat at my desk awaiting my turn, I felt like I was being sent to my execution. Heart pounding, stomach churning, sweat pouring off my brow, I watched with horror as one by one my classmates recited their little speeches. I was sure that each one was far better than anything I could ever hope to do.

When my turn finally came, I would stagger up to the front of the room and mumble a few feeble words while staring down at the floor or up at the ceiling. When this torture was finally over, I would rush back to my seat while trying to ignore the giggling of the class. My dismal performances made me a joke to break up the monotony of dull afternoons. Soon I began to skip school on "speech days."

Socially, things were not much better. I was afraid to ask out any girls because I could not imagine they would ever want to go out with someone like me. I was convinced that most of the guys thought I was a total jerk and didn't like me at all. It was not surprising that I spent a lot of time alone. My best friend during those years was my dog.

As I look back now, I realize the problem was not with my classmates. It was not with my Spanish teacher or anything outside of myself. It was me. I was my own worst enemy.

People tend to look at you the way you look at yourself. If you like yourself and feel good about who and what you are, it shows. On the other hand, if you think of yourself as a zero, people will tend to agree with you. One of the things I can't stress enough is that if you want people to like and respect you, you must first begin by liking and respecting yourself. There is no other way.

How Come I Hate Myself?

You may well wonder why you feel so inferior to others. Why don't you like who you are? Why can't you be your own best friend?

There are many reasons why we get down on ourselves. Sometimes it starts in childhood. One man who is now a famous television actor had a childhood problem with bed-wetting. His parents used to hang his wet underwear outside his bedroom window to humiliate him, hoping to force him to "shape up." Of course, this only made the problem worse and left him with emotional scars that carried into adulthood.

Others have never received praise or recognition for what they have done. No matter what they accomplished, it was never good enough. If they got a "B" they were asked, "Why not an 'A'?" Or else they were compared to some sister or brother who always seemed to do so much better.

Have you ever been compared unfavorably to someone in your own family? Have you ever found yourself striving for recognition and approval that never comes? If so, you are not alone and it helps explain why you don't feel like you amount to much today.

Once we start school, things can get tough very fast. Even in first grade there are some who are weak and some who are strong. There are some who are bright and some who are dull. There are some who are popular and some who are ignored.

You find out very early where you stand and it is pretty hard to change once you get put on the track. Each year becomes a repeat of the last and by the time you reach high school you know so much about failure and defeat that it feels quite natural. It is no wonder that for these, and many other reasons, most young people really don't like themselves very much. That's what I see as I work with them week after week and it makes me sad.

What Can I Do About It?

The real question is not whether young people have a hard time liking themselves or not. The real question is, When you don't like yourself, what can you do about it? Right now.

First, it might help you to know that you are not alone. Many people feel even worse. In my experience working with young people, this is a very common problem. Sometimes it seems almost universal.

It may surprise you to learn that many of the people who seem most sure of themselves, who seem so cocky and conceited, are often the most afraid and unhappy about who and what they are.

I remember one fellow in our high school who I always wanted to be like. His name was Earl and he was on the football and baseball teams. Handsome, well-built, and always stylishly dressed, he was the center of much female attention. As far as I knew, he was unaware that peasants like me even existed.

When I compared myself to Earl and the lucky few who got to hang around him, I felt puny and small. You can imagine my amazement when I really came to know him while we were in some classes together.

We had assigned seats and by chance our teacher placed us beside each other. Over the course of the school year, we talked about the class, sports, and school life in general. After a while, Earl opened up and began to talk about himself.

As he talked about his life and some of the struggles he was facing, I learned that far from being the confident, self-assured person I knew from a distance, he was just like the rest of us in many ways. He too was unsure about many things, especially his brainpower. He was afraid he would be considered just a "dumb jock." And I found living in the fast lane wasn't always as fun or easy as we thought. After a while, I even began to feel sorry for him. I am more convinced than ever that the people who make the most noise and seem to have it all together are often the ones who are struggling the most.

We all tend to look up to someone else and compare ourselves unfavorably to him or her. Once you realize that we all face this, you can begin to stop comparing yourself to others. You can spend more time concentrating on yourself and your own talents and abilities.

God made each person unique. No two people are exactly alike. Each person has his or her own areas to master. If you want to be happy with yourself, the secret is to begin developing those special skills and talents that are yours.

I can almost hear some of you saying now: "Steve, I wish that was true, but I don't have any special talents or abilities. I am just a dull, boring person and there is nothing special about me at all."

Well, let me say as gently as I can, you are dead wrong! Over the years, I have met hundreds, even thousands, of people and every one of them has had something special that they could do. Every one of them has had some quality or strength I admired. I am sure you are not going to be the exception to the rule! Stop selling yourself short. Sit down and really start to think of the things that interest you and that you are good at. Maybe it is a talent for singing or music. Perhaps it's athletics. Maybe it's making friends and having people feel comfortable around you. There are hundreds and thousands of different gifts, and I am convinced every one of us has at least one.

Once you have figured out what your gifts are, start to develop them! One young friend of mine has a talent for playing the piano. She plays it beautifully. However, she also knows that for her talent to develop she must use it. She takes lessons and practices every day. I am so proud of her when she sits down to play. She seems to change from a shy young teenager into a radiant young woman right before my eyes.

I see the same thing happen to others when they stop trying to be someone or something they are not and make the most of what they are. It's almost like magic.

As I was working on this chapter, I interviewed a young woman from our church about these things. She is a senior in high school, quiet and soft-spoken but also confident and poised.

I asked how she came to such peace and comfort with who and what she is. She told me it went back to something she had read in school that basically said, "Imitation is suicide, and to live, you have to be yourself."

To her, being herself means accepting her strengths and developing them. It also means forgiving herself for her weaknesses. Because she does not feel a need to compete with others, she can spend her time making herself special, and believe me, it shows.

The exciting news is that you can do the same thing. If I didn't believe that, I would not try to inspire you with tales of what others have done and are doing now.

The final thing is to begin to develop a winning attitude about yourself. The Bible says that as we think in our hearts, so we are. These words are very true.

If you view yourself as a klutz or a jerk, you will be just that. If all you have ever known is failure and defeat, you will come to expect that and it is what you will receive.

The best way to break the cycle of failure and defeat is to begin to experience victories—even small ones. As you start to achieve little victories, you gradually gain confidence and the sense of being a winner. Soon you expect to win and you will!

Earlier in this chapter, I mentioned my own feelings of self-doubt and inferiority. Rising above such things is not easy. I am not convinced it is something we do alone. I know that I didn't.

My freedom from self-doubt and inferiority came through the love and acceptance of some wonderful friends. One of my ministers taught me that in God's sight each of us is special just as we are. He stressed that point and would not let me forget it.

He encouraged me to find and affirm my strengths and to humbly develop them to the best of my ability. I learned that it was important to find friends who would accept and encourage me for who I was. I was taught to fill each day with three things vital to real happiness and self-contentment: (1) Love for God, (2) love for others, and (3) love for self. These three go together and won't work alone.

If I could talk with you face-to-face, I would leave these same thoughts with you. As we genuinely love God, we come to love ourselves. And as we truly love ourselves, we can love others as well. When we love others, we need no longer view them as enemies, rivals, or superiors. Instead, they become friends and allies, all striving for the same goal—to be the best possible persons we can be.

2

Mirror, Mirror on the Wall, Who Is the Ugliest of Them All?

Do these words sound at all familiar?

> School has been really bad lately. The kids are terrible.... I'm stared upon and snickered at. Other girls call me ugly. I can understand why. At school, my hair is in a ponytail and I don't wear makeup. I'm a real slob. But I go to learn, not for a fashion show.

Sound like the words of some class reject? Sound like the words of people you know who lament about how unattractive or downright ugly they feel themselves to be? Does it even sound like something you might have said about yourself?

Well, my friends, it might interest you to know just who did say those words. Her name is Monika

Schnarre, a 15-year-old brunette who was named Super Model of the World. Her "ugly" face appeared on the cover of *Vogue* magazine and she was also in *Bride's, Mademoiselle, Glamour, Harper's Bazaar,* and *Cover Girl.* For all her glamor and fortune, the six-foot, pouty-mouthed Monika had never even been asked for a date!

I guess this goes to show that even the people who should have no trouble at all, when it comes to looks, have their moments, too. The fear that we don't measure up physically seems to affect us all.

We live in a society that places a high premium on looks. For many, the sole value of a person's worth is measured by what she or he looks like. And because of this, it is not at all surprising that there are such a lot of unhappy people around. The scale and the mirror can become cruel taskmasters.

How do you feel about your looks? Are you comfortable with your physical image or does the sight of a mirror or photograph make you want to vomit? Have the cruel words of family or so-called "friends" about your physical appearance ever cut deep? If you are at all like me, you probably have faced all of these things some time in your life.

The Road Down

I was cute as a little boy, but it was downhill from there. By junior high, I was one of a hundred other faces. I don't recall ever being called cute or handsome then by anyone, even in my own family. At least at that point I was not ugly either. I just sort of blended into the woodwork.

Then things got worse. While playing football in our front yard, I cracked my front tooth in half. My dentist replaced it with a silver cap that stuck out every time I smiled (which soon became a very rare occurrence).

Then the curse of teenage life struck me—acne! Those red splotches and zits that strike fear into the heart of the bravest soul had come upon me. While I don't remember my case being worse than others, to me it was a disaster. I began to avoid mirrors. I also stopped posing for family pictures.

In a desperate attempt to attack the problem, I must have spent hundreds of dollars on Clearisil, Oxy-5, 10, 15 and every other brand name and medical concoction I could find. I washed my face five times a day. Once I scrubbed it so hard that it turned bright red, causing people to ask if I had been burned in a fire!

Adding to all of this, I was skinny. No, mine was not one of those slim, athletic bodies men dream of and work for. Rather, I was what my Mom called "scrawny," like the kid you see in the "Charles Atlas" magazine ads who gets sand kicked in his face. To be charitable, I was not much to look at.

Yet for all my woes, there were others who had it far worse. One girl who was quite heavy had to endure cruel taunts of "beached whale" every time she passed a certain group of guys. Another fellow was called "bubble butt" because of his large rear end. One was nicknamed "Cyrano" because of his large nose. I can't imagine the mentality of some people who throw off such cruel and tasteless remarks.

I wondered if things had changed much since my high school days. Sadly it does not appear that they have. As I talk with my young people, I hear the same tales that I had heard before.

One young girl, who is quite pretty and very talented, carries the nickname "bones" because of her slender figure. In a similar vein, one bright and perky member of my youth group told me her nickname was "carpenter's dream." When I foolishly inquired what this term meant she said softly, "You know, pastor, flat as a board!"

Yet even those who have what seem to be enviable features sometimes are not spared. One young girl who has developed faster than her peers is called "Boobs." She is often the object of much jealousy and unwelcome male exploration. It's not fun.

For those who do battle with the demons of acne, with being too skinny or fat, having big noses or ears, being too tall or too short, not having the "right" hair style or the pretty face, the high school years can be hell.

The real problem is that if enough people tell you that you are unattractive you can start to believe it. Once you start to believe it, then no matter how hard you work to improve yourself you will always see the flaws and imperfections—even if they're not there any more.

Among the most serious health problems of young people are eating disorders such as bulimia and anorexia.

With bulimia, people eat large amounts of food and then force themselves to throw it up. With anorexia they refuse to eat and often can't keep any food down even if they try. Both stem from an extreme fear of being fat. Tragically, in extreme cases these eating disorders can be fatal.

A few years ago there was an extremely popular brother and sister singing team named the Carpenters. Karen and Richard Carpenter produced many hit recordings and seemed destined for a long and successful career. However, Karen was obsessed with a fear of being fat and would not eat. She died of a heart attack caused by anorexia at the age of 32. What a tragic waste of a great talent and life!

Most people who fall victim to these disorders are not fat at all. Some were at one time in the past. Others simply feel fat or were called fat by their peers. Even though they are not fat—and indeed may be seriously underweight—many of these young people still see themselves as chubby, unattractive porkers.

Most of you will never have to face these diseases. However, there are many who feel ugly inside and no matter how hard they try still will feel ugly or unattractive. The past can have quite a hold on us.

Can't You Be More Mature?

Perhaps you have been told that your concern with looks and body image is just a concern of immature teenagers. Don't you believe it!

Adults are every bit as bad, if not worse. We spend millions of dollars on diet programs, tapes, and clinics. (Who do you think lays out the money for ridiculous diet pills that supposedly burn off pounds while you sleep?)

Adults spend millions on clothes, new hairstyles, makeup, and plastic surgery. Adults are obsessed with looking young and sexy. So it is hard for many physically conscious adults to give much encouragement to their struggling kids. What a mess we have made!

You Are What You Are Inside

It's time for some straight talk. The whole system we have of judging people by their looks is ridiculous, cruel, and stupid. Looks never have made a person and they never will. It is high time we start accepting ourselves and others for who we are and rejoice in it.

Are you upset because you are not perfect? Do you

feel that you are too fat or skinny? Do you think your nose too big or your chest too flat? It may surprise you to learn that most models have things that they don't like about their looks. There is no perfect face or body and, when you get right down to it, who cares?

Psychologists have discovered that people who feel attractive inside and like themselves are seen as attractive by others.

I know a young woman named Lin. Flat-chested, plain, and blessed with an odd-shaped nose, she did not stand out as a raving beauty by any means. But she always had plenty of friends and boyfriends and lived a full life.

I asked her once for her secret. With a bright smile lighting up her face she said simply, "Well, I know God didn't give me much of a face or body. But they're what I've got, so I decided to like them!"

Because she liked herself as is, others couldn't help but like her, too. The more glow you have inside, the brighter the glow on the outside.

If you can change or improve something, by all means go ahead. I have seen people transformed by losing some weight or getting a new hairstyle. Simple things like frequent bathing or keeping your teeth clean can do wonders. Some people make themselves unattractive by simple laziness or neglect. Make the most of what you have.

However, if there are things you can't change, then accept them and move on. I knew two girls who were over six feet tall. One was extremely self-conscious about being a "bean pole" and constantly slouched trying to appear shorter. It never worked and she seemed awkward and actually called attention to her height.

The other stood tall, with her shoulders back and her head erect. She walked with grace and poise and never tried to be anything she was not. The guys found her quite attractive and she never seemed too tall at all. The real difference between the two girls was between their ears.

You are special. Accept yourself for you and be you. Smile, walk tall and proud. Take an interest in others. Believe it or not, the people who are most attractive are usually ones who are so busy enjoying themselves that they don't have time to worry about whether they are God's gift to the opposite sex.

Let me level with you. To this day, I am quite average when it comes to looks. I know I will never be in demand as a male model or movie star. I will never stop traffic as I walk up the street. But that's okay, because I like my looks and am happy with them.

Worrying about looks is not something one just "grows out of." It takes a real and genuine effort. It needs to go beyond surface improvements that change the outside but don't touch the inside.

For me, I did all I could to improve my looks. A good dermatologist accomplished wonders for my acne. I had my tooth fixed and treated myself to a new, more becoming hairstyle. But these things were really surface changes and they could only do so much.

The biggest change came on the inside. I made a serious effort to surround myself with people who were not trapped in the "looks game." People like that do exist and they are worth finding. I vowed to stop picking friends based on looks and to search for deeper, more important, qualities. This really made a big difference.

My concern about looks didn't go away overnight and it still bothers me at times. But through the love and support of good friends who know what *really* counts, I have learned to accept myself as I am.

What about you? Can you accept yourself and be happy with who you are? Starting today, try a new way. Smile, stand tall, and be proud. Take your eyes off yourself and that mirror and start developing a genuine interest in others.

If you apply these things and take them seriously, you may not make the cover of *Vogue* magazine. You may not stop traffic when you walk up the street. But I can promise you that you will start to like you and the body God gave you. And once you do that, don't be surprised if people around you start liking you as well!

3

They Can Make or Break You

It was a horrible sight to behold and the pictures of the incident filled our nation's newspapers. Palm Springs, California, during spring break is a place where many young people gather. Usually they are there to socialize and have a good time. But this time things got out of hand and turned ugly.

Many of the youths hurled rocks at police, publicly exposed themselves, and tore the clothing from women. In one scene, which made my local paper, two terrified young women were surrounded by a large group of men and boys who ripped the clothing from their bodies while they huddled, trapped in their car.

Just what kind of beasts are they? How can people be so cruel and gross? Surely they are not the kind of people you and I know. Right? Wrong!

The plain truth is that most of these young men are people just like you and me. They go to school and church and have parents who love them. They don't consider themselves to be evil or vile. To them, it was all in fun.

Do you wonder how people can do things like this, things they would usually never do? Part of the answer is peer pressure.

The presence and support of others have a great deal of influence on us all—for good or evil. In the incidents I described to you, the friends dared each other, helped each other and—because there is safety in numbers—covered for each other. Some people do things in groups that they would never do on their own.

What's the Point?

"Okay, Steve," you may be saying, "I hear you. It sure is an ugly thing you've described. But what's the point of all this? What are you getting at?"

What I am getting at is this. Of all the things that make or break us, of all the things that mold and influence us, of all the things that set us on our road to heaven or hell, few can equal the power of our friends.

Friendships have more influence on teenagers and their behavior, beliefs, and attitudes than do parents, school, church, or any other social factor one can name.

But I don't need to tell you that. Think of how important your friends are to you. Think of how important it is that you be accepted and respected by them. Think how important it is to you to "fit in" and be a part of a group.

Having friends is important and we all need them. But because friends are so important, and because they have so much influence over us, we need to pick them wisely. Few things you ever do will be more vital than picking your friends. Where you are a few years from now will probably depend on who you hang around with today. Indeed, I think it is far more important to pick the right friends than to pick the right courses in school!

The Wrong Turn

One guy I knew in high school was always pretty nice. He was your "average Joe" who worked hard, kept up with his studies, and got along with his family and his friends. I liked him. But when he started to high school he decided to go a different route. He began hanging around some real jerks.

Soon he began to change. It was not long until he was drinking heavily. Later he started using drugs. His grades dropped and he began skipping school.

There was some trouble with the law when he stole a car and crashed it into a tree. The final blow came when he dropped out and just faded away. To this day I don't know what finally did become of him.

As a pastor, I sometimes go to visit people in prison. One thing I hear in talking with inmates is how they got in with the wrong crowd. They thought it couldn't happen to them. I hear the same stories of heartache and wasted lives from other people in many areas of life. It does matter whom we associate with!

It Goes Both Ways

While it is true that the wrong friends can drag us down, it is also true that the right friends can lift us up and help make us better.

Over the years, I have been blessed with some really good friends who stick by me through anything and everything. They are like family to me. They have helped me get through dark times and to be where I am today. I am forever grateful to them.

There's an old song by the Beatles that says, "I can get by with a little help from my friends" and I know that is true. How about you?

When you have true friends who can support and encourage you, and help make you the best you can be, you've got a treasure worth more than gold.

One local high school near my home recently began a support group for young people from broken homes. While helping each other to build new lives, the young people become real and deep friends.

One member said of her group: "It's nice to be able to talk to people who know where I'm coming from. It's nice to be able to listen to others with the same problems and help them."

Another said of her experience: "I like having the chance to talk to people who might understand. We have something in common and it's possible to get advice, condolence, sympathy, and support."

Those qualities—advice, sympathy, and support—are what real friendships are all about. Whether it is getting through dark times like death or divorce, or celebrating good times, good friends can make all the difference in the world.

What Do I Look for in a Friend?"

Finding someone to hang around with is easy. Finding people with the qualities that make for real and genuine friendship requires more work, but it is worth it.

What would I look for in a friend? As I think of it, several qualities come to mind. See if they match up with yours.

First, a real friend is *genuine.* This means that the person is really your friend and not nice to your face and cruel behind your back. Although the term isn't used much any more, "fair weather friends" are still quite common.

I know people who would talk to you and be with you as long as their "click group" wasn't around. They were as nice as anyone could be. However, if it seemed that a better group opened up, they turned cold and were quickly gone. This is not real friendship.

A second major quality is *trust.* Any lasting relationship must be based on trust. If you can't trust a person, he or she really isn't a friend. Trust is at the core of real friendship.

I have a friend named Big John. We have known each other since high school. If John tells me it's raining outside, I reach for my umbrella. When Big John comes to my house, I don't have to worry about my money, my wife, or my dog. I trust him with everything I have and that is how it should be with friends.

Can you trust your friends? Can you believe them when they tell you things? Are they honest and true? Or, do you constantly catch them in lies and deceit? If you find your "friends" fail here, perhaps it's time to start seriously looking for some new friends.

A third vital quality is *acceptance.* Real friends accept each other as they are. Each of my friends is different. Some are quite good looking, while others are plain. Some are very academic, while others barely finished high school. Some are athletic and sports oriented; others couldn't tell the difference between a football and a Frisbee.

Yet, each of them is special to me. I accept them just as I hope that they accept me. Each of us is a unique creation and we all have good points and bad points. I am sure there are things about me that my friends consider odd and there are things about them I consider odd. The reason we are friends is that we don't let these things bother us or stand in the way of our friendship.

A real friend lets you be you. If you have to put on an act or wear a mask around people, they're probably not real friends. Have you ever noticed how when you're with certain people you have to think carefully before you say or do anything so they won't laugh or get mad at you? Have you ever found yourself saying and doing things that really aren't you, just to try to fit in with some group or person? Around real friends, you won't have to do this. They fit like a comfortable pair of shoes.

A fourth quality is *encouragement*. Real friends encourage and root for each other.

I once saw some events in the Special Olympics. These young athletes are all handicapped in one way or another. Yet they still love to participate in sports and give it their all.

The difference I saw in these events was that many of these young people were really helping and encouraging each other. One young man in a wheelchair stopped short of the finish line during the race he was in and waited for his friend to catch up so they could cross the line together.

Others stood cheering loudly, encouraging those whose strength was failing or who were about to quit. Here there were no losers—everyone won. That is real friendship!

Life can be tough. At times we are hit by blows that make us feel like giving up. A real friend is one who comes with an uplifting word or sign of support. Many people owe their success and position in life to the help and encouragement given by caring friends. Others wouldn't even be alive today were it not for the friends who helped in dark times.

The last quality I want to look at is *enrichment*. I said earlier that real friends should bring out the best in each other. Some friendships do that; some don't.

The mark of a real friendship is when we care enough to confront each other about things that are wrong. Enrichment goes beyond just accepting or encouraging; it includes challenging. It can be risky, but sometimes it's the only way.

Once I had to confront one of my best friends about something he was doing that was just not like him at all. He was constantly making crude sexual jokes and had lustful comments about almost every available female he saw. Soon he was doing this in front of many of his other friends and acquaintances. He was starting to act like a real jerk. Some people began to avoid him while others were talking behind his back.

I was afraid to say anything for fear he would get mad. Yet, I knew this was not really what he was like. I could tell he was trying to get attention and affection in the wrong way.

Finally, I decided that if I really cared I would have to confront him. When I went to talk to him about it I was so nervous that my stomach hurt and I got a headache. I was sure he was going to tell me to go to hell, but I couldn't watch or listen to this any more.

Much to my amazement, he listened and thanked me for caring enough to face him. He admitted that he felt bad about the jokes, but thought they were what others wanted from him.

Once he saw how he was really coming across and what was happening, he didn't like it at all. He made some real changes over the next few months and became much nicer to be around. I like to think our little talk had something to do with that.

I know over the years there have been times when I have acted like a total fool. I have appreciated friends who cared enough and had the courage to tell me about it to my face.

Real friends can also enrich us by bringing new dimensions into our lives. I had a friend who shared with me his knowledge of hiking and another who taught me about racquetball. Others have led me to discoveries and new experiences in many different areas of life. Every true friend I have has enriched my life in one way or another and made it better.

What do your friends do for you? Do you learn new things from them? Do you feel good after you are with them or do you find yourself regretting things you have said or done? It's been said that a true friend helps bring out the best that's in you and I believe that's true.

Well let's sum it up. The five qualities we have talked about are all marks of a real friend. Friends who are genuine, trustworthy, accepting, encouraging, and enriching are special. They are more valuable than money or cheap popularity, which many of us pursue so desperately. If you find them, don't let them go!

How Can I Make Friends?

This question has been asked by people of all ages throughout history. Dale Carnegie made millions of dollars from a book he wrote called, *How to Win Friends and Influence People.* It sold tens of thousands of copies to people just like you and me trying to find the secret of friendship. Other authors and experts have written books, developed courses and seminars, and prepared lectures and speeches on this subject as well. Some are good and helpful; some are trash and not worth the paper they are printed on. But this great wealth of material shows the need that exists. Remember, in your struggle to find real friendships you are not alone.

I am not going to even try to write a quick "how to" course on friendships in a few pages of this book. To deal with that subject would require a whole book in itself.

Still, I will close this chapter with these thoughts. Every quality that you are looking for in your friends, they look for in you. We tend to get back what we send out.

You want your friends to be genuine. You want to know they are the same whether they are with you or not. Well, are you genuine? Do you talk about your friends behind their backs? Are you a friend they can count on? Think about it!

You want friends you can trust. Can your friends trust you? Do they know you to be honest and reliable? If you can't be trusted, it will be hard to find friends to trust.

You want friends who accept you for what you really are. Do you accept your friends for what they are? Do you love them and care about them even if they are not perfect?

You want friends who encourage you and help you. Do you encourage your friends and help them? Do you rejoice when something good happens to your friends or do you think the good things should happen to you? Do you have time for your friends or are you too busy? If you aren't there for your friends, you may find that they won't be there for you.

You want friends who enrich you and make you better. What kind of influence do you have on your friends? Do you care enough to confront them when you need to? Do you care enough to want to help them be the best they can be? Real friendship is based on giving. If you give out your best, that is what you will get back.

Now, I want you to do something. Look at the questions we have just raised. Then, put this book down and think really hard about them. Be honest with yourself and ask how you rate.

If you are like me, you probably found some areas you need to work on. That's okay. The important thing is to face up to your faults and start working on them today!

Friendship is an art you can learn. Now you know what to look for in friends. But more importantly, you know what it takes to be a friend. Try it and see.

4

Just Someone to Call My Own

I look in the mirror and ask, "What's wrong with me?" Is it my figure? My nose? My braces? Then I wonder if I'm just too boring or what.... No guys ever pay attention to me. I wonder if there's anyone who wants to be with me?—Sandy, age 15

I don't know what's wrong. Lately my boyfriend and I fight all the time and now he's spending a lot more time with his other friends. It didn't start out like this.... I'm really afraid I'm going to lose him.—Jenny, age 16

Sometimes it hurts so bad! I wish I'd die. I think about her all the time and I know I will never love anyone else. I can't eat. I can't sleep. I just want her back—like it was before.—Jeff, age 17

Few things in life bring us more joy—or more pain—than our special relationships. This is especially true when it comes to having a boyfriend or girlfriend. Boyfriend or girlfriend problems rank high on the list of teenage concerns.

Whether it's the pain of wanting someone special to be with and care for, or the times when nothing seems to work and the two of you are fighting, or when that special relationship is over and you're trying to pick up the pieces of your heart and go on, boyfriend or girlfriend concerns have a way of dominating our thoughts and feelings.

In this chapter, we have much to cover. First, I want to talk with those who feel left out, who really don't have anyone special. That can be tough.

Then I want to talk to those who have a special someone, but have found that it's not all that you thought it would be. Maybe things are pretty rocky right now. Is there anything that can be done? Is your relationship worth saving?

Finally, I want to talk to those who carry the pain of a breakup. Anytime a deep relationship ends, whether you chose to end it or you were told good-bye, it brings real grief. Sometimes the pain is so deep that, as one popular song goes, "It cuts like a knife." It's hard enough for adults to experience. For a teenager, it can be devastating.

I won't offer any easy answers or cheap solutions. You're too smart to fall for those. What I will do is try to help you sort through what's really happening. Because I have been where you may be now, I want to help.

What's Wrong with Me?

While I was writing this book, I interviewed young people about their problems and concerns. Many worried about being left out in life, feeling unwanted and lonely because it seemed no one of the opposite sex really desired them.

Some had dated, but found that nothing seemed to click. Promises like "I'll call you" or "Let's get together again soon" were getting awfully old.

Others were sick of spending Saturday nights watching TV or playing with the cat. Hearing their friends talk about the special things they did with their boyfriend/girlfriend was driving them crazy. Some felt as though they were the only person on earth who had no one special and were ashamed and embarrassed about it.

I think of Sandy. Dark-eyed, stylishly dressed, and strikingly pretty, she would figure to be the object of much male attention. Friendly and sincere, she did have some good girl and guy friends. But, the thing she wanted most, she admitted in a quiet voice, was a real boyfriend. "It's weird" she said, "People want to be my friend. They say I'm cute, or nice, or fun to be with, but I hardly ever get asked out. It's starting to bother me a lot."

Then there's Amy. She dates quite often and many guys like her, but nothing seems to last. She wonders if she is too boring, or too picky, or maybe just unlucky. Each time she goes out, she hopes that this might be the start of something special. So far, each time she has come home empty.

Rich has his own way of dealing with things. When his friends or parents ask if he is dating anyone, he casually replies with some remark about "playing the field" or "not wanting to be tied down."

He is quick to point out that he doesn't want or need a girlfriend and sometimes ridicules his friends who have one. His boasting and flippancy are really just a weak cover-up. The truth is, each girl he's asked out has said "no." Deep inside it bothers him a lot!

However we choose to deal with it, feeling unwanted can be tough. Some, like Sandy, wonder why no one asks them out. Others, like Amy, wonder why they can't seem to hold on to anyone. And still others, like Rich, hide the bitter disappointment of rejection behind bold remarks or an "I could care less" attitude. I suspect we all have felt and acted a bit like each of them at some time or other.

If you have ever felt unwanted or incomplete because you don't have someone, you are not alone! Many around you feel the same way. Some simply hide it better than others.

Whatever your situation today, don't panic. One of the reasons many people don't have a special person is that they put such pressure on themselves and others that things can't help but fail.

Some develop an air of desperation about themselves that others can actually feel. Because their own self-worth is tied in to having a boyfriend or girlfriend, they tend to feel bad about themselves if they don't have one. And when you feel bad about yourself, others soon start agreeing with you!

Having a boyfriend or girlfriend can be very special. It can lead to a lot of good times and new experiences, but it can never take the place of genuine self-love and inner strength. When you like yourself and feel good about who you are, you're happy—with or without a special person.

Once you take the pressure off, you can begin to enjoy life for what it is. If you have someone—great! Enjoy your relationship and be glad for it.

But if you are completely unattached, don't panic or get down. Being willing to take each day and live it to the fullest is a mark of real maturity. Life goes on all around us, but we must be willing to live it! You can miss a lot while you're waiting.

It may well be that your special relationship comes when you are not looking for it. As you keep active and open, as you are friendly to all (not just those you want to date), as you keep positive and cheerful, you place yourself in a position for wonderful things to happen.

When you go out looking, you often come up empty. When you relax and do what you like to do in life—regardless of whether you see yourself meeting someone or not—the most special relationships often sneak up on you and take you by surprise! Life can be fun that way.

Nothing Works Anymore!

Even when we have someone, life has its disappointing moments. Those who expected all their problems to disappear once they found a special relationship are shocked to discover that new problems often surface and many old ones are still there.

Some relationships start off wonderfully. We feel alive with the newness of discovery. We picture an endless time of movies and dinner dates, of bowling and pizza. The phone rings and we hurry to answer. "It might be Jim!" We write little notes and buy cute gifts. We say that this is real. "Why, it feels like I've known her all my life!"

Sound familiar? But all too soon the other side emerges. "Mr. Right" gets super jealous if you even talk to another guy. "Miss Perfect" doesn't like your friends and thinks you spend too much time with them. Sometimes you find yourselves feeling bored with each other. Why, there are even times when you feel like breaking up!

The fact is that any relationship—good or bad—has its down times. Once the novelty of having a boyfriend/girlfriend has worn off, the relationship undergoes a new period of testing and examination.

Sometimes we find our friend is possessive or jealous. Other times, we may discover that she lies or has a violent temper. Then there are those times when we find, to our great dismay, that we really don't have much in common or we have grown apart. Some relationships survive these times; some don't.

Only the Perfect Need Apply

All of us have faults and failings. So does your boyfriend or girlfriend. No one person or relationship is perfect. People who spend their lives looking for the perfect person or relationship end up empty and alone.

Maintaining your special relationship takes work. It requires you to accept each other as you are and to be honest and straight with one another. Any relationship that lasts beyond a few dates must be cultivated like a lush garden. Otherwise the weeds of boredom, envy, and laziness will choke and finally kill it.

You need to know what is important to you. Personally, I could not date someone who constantly lied or was possessive and jealous. These things turn me off completely.

On the other hand, I wouldn't care whether she had blond hair or brown, whether she were rich, poor, or middle class.

When it comes to deciding what to do about faults and failings, what is important to you? It is one thing to be too picky. It is quite another to have a realistic knowledge of what you need and expect from a relationship. Some things are important. You must be the judge.

Some relationships can be saved with hard work and genuine depth of mutual feeling. Some just don't have it and are best put to rest. Often, only time will show what we really have.

My first real girlfriend was a lovely girl named Karin. Blue-eyed, athletic, and attractive without being snobbish, she was everything I ever dreamed of in a girlfriend. Soon, I was deeply "in love." All I could think about was Karin, night and day.

The first two months were great. I couldn't have been happier. But then my feet hit the ground and I came back to earth. So did Karin.

We both discovered that there were many areas of our lives in which we were completely different! Our beliefs about religion, our choice of friends—even how much time we felt we should spend together.

We tried to work things out. We tried hard, for neither of us wanted to break up over minor reasons. But in the end, we both concluded that our relationship could not go on. We broke off over things that were of real importance to us. It took time for us to see that these were important.

Some Suggestions for Better Relationships

Give your relationships time. If you have worked on things and they keep getting worse, time will show whether to quit or to try harder. Time will show whether you have been drawn together by mutual affection or because you just don't want to be alone. However slowly, time does reveal the truth. Be patient and open. Let it work for you.

Be honest. I can't stress this enough. If you don't like someone, don't use her or string him along. It is all too easy to lie or act in ways we really don't feel because we don't want to hurt another person. And cheating on each other can cause a great deal of pain. If you've decided to date someone else, have the decency to tell your partner first.

Be sure to communicate. Talk about things as they are. You may think that by ignoring problems they will go away. They won't. Sooner or later problems must be faced. If you wait until they become crises, it may be too late. Any relationship that lasts is based on trust and open communication. This is true whatever your age.

Give space. A good relationship works because each person wants to be involved in it. If you cling to someone like a vine or chain him to you as an object not to be let out of your sight, your relationship is doomed to fail.

All of us need space. We need time for ourselves and for our other friends and interests. Relationships that don't recognize this become suffocating and quickly end. If your relationship is real, your times apart will make the times together even better. If it's not, forcing it with tears and chains of constant togetherness will only make for two very unhappy prisoners of love. As one popular song goes, "If you love somebody, set them free!"

She's Gone

It hurts. You invested so much of yourself in your relationship and now it's over. The pain inside won't leave. You may not feel like eating or you may want to eat all the time. You may not be able to sleep or you may spend the whole day in bed.

When a relationship ends, it can shake us to the core. I don't think that many adults know—or they have forgotten—how bad the pain of a teenage breakup can be. Sayings like "There are plenty of fish in the sea" or, "It's only puppy love—you'll get over it," miss the point entirely and are insensitive and cruel.

When a loss occurs in our lives, we go through a period of mourning. It's almost like a death. And whether the relationship was ended by your choice or against your wishes, real pain is involved.

I have been on both sides of this. Once I had to break off a relationship with a very special person. We had even talked of marriage. Then things began to sour. The thought of telling her it was over and causing her pain made me sick in body and mind.

I had no appetite and lost ten pounds. I would go to bed early and sleep until one or two the next afternoon. My grades dropped and I found it hard to concentrate on anything. I avoided my friends and family and even was mad at our dog. Each day was torture. At that point in my life, I did not want to hear about "puppy love" or "other fish in the sea!" Such words didn't help me at all.

They don't help much when you're being dropped either. There were times when I was given what I refer to as "the speech." This was that dreaded conversation which a girl I really liked began by saying, "Steve, you're a nice guy, but...." When the speech was over, basically what I was told was "good-bye." That was not fun at all!

Some Thoughts

Allow room for pain. Whatever side you come from—breaking it off or being sent away—your pain is real. It's also normal. Any relationship that is worth anything should be missed when it's over. Give yourself time to hurt. It may seem to take forever, but you really can't rush healing. Be patient and know it's okay to hurt.

Don't cling. Sometimes we are tempted to cling to a lost love. It really won't work. Temper tantrums or suicide threats or nasty notes do not help the cause. Relationships kept together by fear or guilt aren't happy ones at all. I don't know of any relationship that has ever been saved by begging or desperate attempts to win sympathy.

Talk it out. Don't go into a shell. Find someone you trust and share your feelings. It may be God, a counselor, your pastor, your parents, some close friend—but by all means find someone. As you share your pain, you will gain new strength from the love and support of people who care.

As I was writing this book, something happened in the life of a young woman from our church—let's call her Jean—that illustrates this very thing.

Young, attractive, and full of excitement and anticipation, she came to my office to talk about getting married. She and Tom, her boyfriend of five years, were engaged and she wanted me to perform the ceremony.

As she talked with great joy about her relationship with Tom, and the hopes and dreams she had for their marriage, I could not help but share in her excitement and enthusiasm. Soon we scheduled the wedding date and reserved the church for that day. We agreed to meet soon to go over the exact details of the wedding service. She was happy and so was I.

However, just a few weeks later, a sobbing and distraught Jean called to tell me that Tom had, without any warning, broken their engagement. The wedding was off. Hurt and uncertain of what to do next, she asked if she could come to my office and talk.

When she arrived, I could quickly see the toll this painful event had taken upon her. Shoulders slumped and eyes wet with tears, she looked defeated and alone.

Gone was the bright young woman that had joyfully scheduled her wedding just a few weeks earlier. I felt pity and compassion for her, but wondered what I could possibly say in this time of loss and grief.

For quite awhile, she talked about her pain and feelings of rejection as well as her fear of the unknown future. But, even as she talked, I could sense that in this very hurt young woman there was also a great inner strength.

She was deeply religious and had a strong personal relationship with God. As she talked about that and also of the love she felt from her family and friends, she seemed to gain new power right before my eyes. When she stood up to leave she said with some conviction that she was going to be all right.

Shortly after that conversation, she took a job in a large Eastern city and moved away. She promised to write when she was established and let me know how she was doing. I hoped she would.

A few months later, a wonderful letter arrived from Jean. I want to share part of it with you. To me, it is a letter of victory and hope.

> I am doing very well. Thanks to a wonderful job—new friends ... but mostly all the support I received from friends that prayed for me and talked with me.
>
> My work with the extension office gets me out and meeting people daily, plus manages to keep my mind off myself. In my spare time, I volunteer teaching English to Asian refugees. I also have a new set of friends with whom I take weekend trips to the bay and beach.
>
> God does have plans better than we imagine! I am doing things I never dreamed I'd have the ability or opportunity to do. I was selected for an internship in Utah.... It's hard to believe that I must move once again—but I am positive I can do it!
>
> I'll keep in touch as time goes by. I mostly wanted to

thank you for sharing and caring—and to let you know I am happy.

Take care,
Jean

My friend, Jean, is special and she is strong. But she is no more special nor is she stronger than you. With God's help and the love of family and friends, she made it just like she said she would. So can you.

5

How Far Did You Go?

I always wanted to save myself for that one special guy. I know it sounds corny, but I dreamed about wearing a white gown and still being a virgin on my wedding night. I wanted the first time to be beautiful and full of love. Instead it was quick, messy, and painful. I feel used and ashamed.—Lori, age 15

After it was over, I remember thinking: "Is that it? It seems a lot different in the movies."—Sean, age 16

To me, sex is a very personal thing. I want to decide when to have it and not until I really feel ready. Until then, I'll just say, "No ."—Jenny, age 16

The teenage years are times when most of us begin making major sexual decisions. This is a serious time and the consequences of our decisions go far beyond the moment. They have a profound affect on our present and future happiness and adjustment.

Of all the pressures that come to bear on a person, few can equal the power of young love. Sex is a beautiful and wonderful thing, but in many ways it is like a fire. Used properly and controlled, it is a blessing. Used wrongly or out of control, it destroys and becomes a curse.

When the Heat Is On

Most teenagers face some major forces that drive them toward sexual activity. Each of us goes through certain stages and reasons for getting physically involved. See if you can find which stage—or stages—you are dealing with in your life.

Stage One: Curiosity

Let's face it. Boys and girls have a natural curiosity about their bodies and, to some extent, sex itself. Young children often check each other out and compare their bodily development with great interest. Games like "playing doctor" or "post office" are probably part of the experience of most of us. Curiosity is a natural part of growing up.

As we move into our teenage years, this curiosity changes. It moves from the simple innocence of discovering that there is a difference between boys and girls to a more active desire to know about the mysteries of sex itself.

We place posters of our favorite music and movie stars on our bedroom walls. We find ourselves talking more and more about sex to our friends. We hope the movies we watch will have at least one hot love scene. Our thoughts become increasingly focused on sex.

We wonder, "What's it all about?" "What does it feel like?" "Is it like we see in the movies or read about in books?" "When are we old enough or ready?" We have so many questions and so few answers.

As we mature physically, we find that our curiosity becomes even stronger and at times can seem all-consuming. We feel drives and desires we didn't even know we had.

When I was about thirteen years old, my friends and I found an old pile of men's magazines which someone had discarded in the woods behind my house. We seized these magazines and hid them like a special treasure in our secret clubhouse. There we would go to read and study them at least a hundred times!

Until then, we had never even seen such magazines—much less the things they depicted. Page after page contained explicit photos of naked men and women posing in erotic embraces and scenes, articles and letters describing in graphic detail the pleasure of sex, and advertisements for sexual products and games. These girlie magazines took us to a new realm of curiosity and desire.

As we drooled over the sights, we each wanted to learn everything about sex—and soon! We talked about girls we could find to "do it" with us. We wondered what a naked woman really looked like compared to the ones in our magazine. For the moment at least, the most important thing in our world was to experience sex.

The simple truth is that while we may have been physically ready to have sex we were far from ready emotionally or spiritually. We were kids, and I am glad that we did not act on our youthful passions.

However, I must confess that only fear, guilt, and a basic lack of opportunity prevented us from premature sexual activity which could have had lasting consequences. In this stage, there was not a desire to love or be involved in a committed relationship. Our burning desire was to know and explore the great unknown regardless of the consequences—most of which we were completely ignorant of!

That experience taught me much about the tremendous power of curiosity. It never really goes away and in many ways it is difficult to call it just a stage. Are we ever not curious?

Stage Two: Pressure

Today, you face things I never dreamed of facing. Scenes and situations that my friends and I found in dirty magazines hidden in the woods, you can see at the movie theater or at home on your V.C.R. Music, magazines, and TV all urge you to experience sex for yourself. You're pushed and pulled to try it. Everywhere you turn the message is clear, that sex is the ultimate "adult" experience. Any normal young person is bound to wonder what it's all about.

Just natural curiosity is hard enough to resist. When you add the sophisticated prompting of the advertisers and entertainment industry, the temptation and desire to experience what others talk about can be overwhelming. I know it can be tough.

Curiosity is largely an inner desire and prompting. In this second stage, the pressure comes from boyfriends or girlfriends, our peer group, so-called "sex experts," and society. Major pressures come from the outside and try to cause you to change your attitudes, beliefs, and behaviors.

Numerous "lines" are used, many of them as old as the hills. Do any of these sound familiar to you?

"Are you afraid or just frigid?"

"All of our friends do it. Why can't we?"

"I really love you and I'll be with you forever!"

"If you won't, I'll have to find someone who will."

All of us fear losing things we value, and one of these is our pride. Many times you will notice that the appeal is made to your ego. You may find your manhood or womanhood challenged. Questions are raised about your sexual abilities or competence. Many are made to feel embarrassed and ashamed "still to be a virgin at 16."

We may fear losing our boyfriend or girlfriend to someone else. "Why should he stay with me if he can't get what he needs? I know he is going to drop me if I don't put out soon." We fear being labeled as "cold" or "straitlaced" and passed by in the dating scene. We fear being cast out.

Sadly, pressure can come from places you least expect. It's rough when your best friend tells you how great sex is and pushes you to try it for yourself. The more sexually active your peers are, or claim they are, the more pressure is put on you to conform, even if you are not at all ready.

One form of pressure that can be extremely annoying and intimidating is physical. Touches, kisses, and fondling against one's will can be unwelcome reminders of how gross some people can be.

Penny is fifteen and knows about this from her own painful experience. Attractive, with nice legs and a full figure, she became the target of much pinching and poking from the boys. At first, having her fanny pinched or her breasts squeezed was simply an annoyance, something that immature kids tend to do. She hoped it would pass.

Later, things became more than just annoying. The harassment became a daily ordeal and more prolonged, suggestive, and vulgar. She began to feel quite afraid. One afternoon, as she was walking home from school, she was forced behind some large bushes by three older boys who tore off her shirt and bra. Only her terrified screams for help saved her from being more severely assaulted or raped.

Her experience left her shaken and fearful of men. She felt guilty and dirty, as if she had brought it all on herself by dressing the wrong way or walking home alone on that warm fall afternoon. She seriously considered quitting school and required counseling to deal with her trauma. The whole experience was like one long nightmare.

Penny's case is extreme, but she is certainly not alone. Many girls—and some guys—have been touched, pinched, and fondled against their will. While at times such attention may even seem flattering, it soon becomes annoying and harmful.

Physical pressure can range from the kid who pinches your rear as you walk up the stairs, to a date whose hand starts out at your knee and moves steadily north during the movie.

Dates who happen to "accidentally" brush against your breasts or hold you a bit too tightly on a social occasion are another example of physical pressure. It is so common that you may take such touching as normal, yet it is really a violation of your body and shows real lack of restraint and respect. You have a right not to be touched or violated in any way. Your body is your own and no one, not even a friend, has the right to touch it without your consent.

Stage Three: Desire
We know that curiosity about the bodies of others and the pleasures of sex are powerful forces. We don't

doubt that emotional or physical pressure can be overwhelming. However, neither curiosity nor external pressure is the main factor in becoming sexually active. The most significant reason is our own desire—those times when we don't want to say "no."

When a relationship becomes special and you're in love, there is a natural desire for physical intimacy and closeness. You want to share your thoughts, feelings, and—as the relationship deepens—your bodies with each other.

Such a desire for closeness is natural. Anyone who has ever been in love knows such feelings well. Stephanie, fifteen years old, said it this way: "My boyfriend and I don't 'have sex' or 'screw.' We make love, and there is a big difference. We love each other and want to please each other any way that we can. When you really love someone you shouldn't have to hold back."

Bob, age sixteen, had this to say: "I wouldn't sleep with just anybody. I think sex is wrong if it is just physical. But when you love someone and they love you, it's beautiful. Sex shows by action what can't be expressed in words."

The burning desire to give and receive physical love is much more intense than the passion produced by curiosity or pressure. Those who say teenagers are too young to feel genuine love, and the desire it brings, are quite wrong! You can be in love and the physical drives that go with that experience are real.

Many of the young people I talked with, who were sexually involved, said they had not started having sex until they fell in love. Some who were not at present sexually active said they might be if they truly loved the person.

While having casual sex was frowned upon, quite a few felt that it was very hard to say "No" to sex in a committed relationship. Many young people were not sure why anyone should want to say "No." As a factor in sexual decisions, the power of desire is the strongest of them all.

It's All So Confusing!

It is never easy to face difficult and major decisions. Deciding if and when to become sexually active is one of the most important decisions you will ever face in your whole life. I urge you to think about it now, as you read this book, rather than during a moment of passion.

Deciding such a matter is an extremely personal step and you need to be able to think and reason for yourself. I don't want to lecture or preach to you, but I do hope you will consider some important things that many overlook.

First, not everyone is "doing it." Many young people have the mistaken belief that every other teenager in the world is sexually active. They hear the bragging of friends and see the way sex is portrayed in movies and on TV and feel isolated and alone. Often they may engage in sex just to feel like part of the group.

The fact is that many teenagers are virgins by choice and many of those who brag the most about their sex life are, too. Studies show that many of the brightest and best teenagers are not sexually active and never have been.

Even if everyone else is sexually active, you must still decide for yourself. You have your own beliefs, values, and personality. Never make a decision based on what someone else is doing or claiming to be doing. Such a decision may be totally wrong for you. Don't sacrifice your beliefs to conform to others. It's not worth the price.

What About Natural Curiosity?

Yes, the desire to know can seem overpowering, but curiosity is a poor reason to become sexually active. People are not like laboratory animals on which to experiment. If we use people to find out what sex is about, we lower them, we cheapen sex, and we lower ourselves.

Sex should be discovered with someone you care for and are committed to, not someone you use and dispose of.

Consider the Risks

The risks involved in becoming sexually active are considerable and must not be ignored. The most obvious risk—but by no means the only one—is an unplanned pregnancy, which I will talk about in the next chapter.

Another risk is physical disease. Venereal diseases are not just "adult problems." Each year, thousands of teenagers contract them and will suffer significant physical and emotional pain. With casual sex, such a risk is always present.

The emotional risks are even greater. Few experiences are more painful than giving everything to someone you have come to love and trust and then being rejected. Many young people have expected sex to deepen their relationship only to discover that it may have helped to end it. Waiting for a phone call that never comes or being ignored by your ex-lover as you pass in the hall can be devastating.

Many people have found that moments of intimacy they thought were private and special were being broadcast like a sporting event. Reputations have been destroyed and trust damaged badly by insensitive clods who used sex as a game to brag about to their friends. What is your reputation and self-respect worth to you? Only you can answer that.

Is This the Right Time?

Even if you are comfortable with the thought of being sexually active, are you sure this is the right time for it? Sex may be beautiful and good at one point in life and wrong and harmful at another. Much of this difference depends on maturity, responsibility, and commitment.

Even older teens are still growing and maturing. Something as deep and significant as the sexual experience often requires greater degrees of responsibility and commitment than most teens possess. It is okay to wait until you have developed the capabilities to meet the demands sexuality brings on a relationship. Indeed, it requires much more maturity to wait patiently until you are really ready than to try to prove your adulthood by premature sexual involvement.

Is This the Right Person?

Even if you are sure you possess the emotional maturity to handle sexual involvements, are you sure this is the right person to be involved with?

Some have sex casually with anyone they like and happen to feel attracted to. Others are more selective and tend to limit their sexual involvements. Most of the young people I have encountered are extremely selective and would only be sexually involved with someone they love and plan to be with forever.

You may feel in love and plan on being with your boyfriend or girlfriend for life. Sex may seem so good and right. What is the value or need for waiting?

The sad truth is most teenage relationships do not last forever. Indeed, I read that the average man or woman will have between six and twelve serious relationships from the time they begin dating until they marry. Most fall in love several times. If you only had sex when you were in love, you could well have twelve or more partners!

My first and only sexual partner was my wife, Karen. But I was in love several times before I met her. At least twice, I was sure I was going to marry the girl I was dating at the time. But that was not the case.

The Buck Stops Here!

Ultimately, the decision is yours. No one else can make it for you, nor should they. You must—and will—live with the consequences and the joys of the decisions you make.

When it comes to something as sacred as sex, don't let someone else decide for you! Not this book, not your friends, not even your boyfriend or girlfriend should be allowed to make the decision for you. You must come to know what is right for you. After all, you live with yourself every day of your life. If you are not true to what you really are and believe, that can seem like a long and unhappy time!

In my own life, I found sex was well worth waiting for. Sharing it in a committed, permanent marriage relationship meant freedom from guilt, shame, or fear of rejection. It has been a real blessing and joy. My sincere hope is that it will be all this for you and more!

6

Oh My God, Not Me!

Meet Jenny. She is seventeen and in many ways might be described as a typical teenager. She likes to party with her friends. She likes to listen to music and watch television. She loves pizza and hates algebra. She's been saving her money for college and hopes to be a lawyer someday.

But all that will have to wait. She doesn't have much time to party or listen to music right now. She doesn't worry much about algebra either. She's no longer in school. For Jenny, being a mother is a full-time job.

Sue, stunned and barely comprehending, listens to the words of her doctor as if they were a sentence of death. "Pregnant, how can I be pregnant? My God, I'm only fourteen years old!" She looks at her mother, then back to her doctor, hoping it's all a bad dream. Deep inside she knows it's not.

Tom is eighteen. Until this year he was one of the best students at Norwood High. Tall, muscular, and athletic, he excelled in football, basketball, and track. He planned on going to college on a full scholarship.

This year, however, there will be no football, basketball, or track. There will be no college—at least for quite a while. Instead, Tom's day begins at three each morning when he climbs into his battered old pickup truck to deliver newspapers to the city merchants six days a week.

Finishing his route, he then goes to work each morning and afternoon at his father's store. In the evenings, he tries to spend some time with his girlfriend, Cindy, and their son, Tommy. Being a father at eighteen doesn't leave much time for a social life or things like football, basketball, or track. Sometimes, when he is all alone, Tom can't help crying.

Jenny, Sue, and Tom are real people. They are probably, in many ways, just like you. What they face is something faced by millions of teenagers each year—teen pregnancy.

Every year over one million teenage girls become pregnant in the United States. For them—and for the fathers of their children—life is changed forever.

There is no typical teenage pregnancy. Teenage pregnancy happens to the rich and poor, to honor students and to dropouts, to prom queens and wallflowers. It is no respecter of race, creed, or position.

Some of you reading this chapter may think it can't happen to you. Some of you may fear that it will. Some of you may be pregnant now or have been in the past.

Whatever your situation, please don't tune out. This chapter may have something to say to you. Nothing you will ever face will change your life as much as bringing a child into the world.

When it comes at the right time, parenthood can fulfill your deepest longing and lifelong dreams. At the wrong time, it can be the start of a nightmare that never seems to end. The time you spend reading and thinking now may have much to do with the course your life will take from here.

How Can This Be?

What is happening? Why do one million teenage girls become pregnant each year? What are the reasons and what can be done? Can it happen to me?

Each day parents, educators, and people from all walks of life grapple with these problems. Each day teenagers, just like you, live them out.

Several reasons have been given for why so many teenagers become pregnant. No single answer explains all teenage pregnancies, but these seem to be the main reasons for what is taking place. What do you think are the main reasons? As you read, compare your reasons to my list.

Reason One: Sexual Ignorance and Misinformation

We live in a society which prides itself on being sexually liberated and open. Yet, there is much ignorance about sex and pregnancy among teenagers—and even among adults.

One in three single women in their 20s has been pregnant at least once. These women are supposedly mature, enlightened, and educated. Yet, they still have many unplanned pregnancies. Reasons for unplanned adult pregnancies and for teenage pregnancies are often the same—ignorance and misinformation.

Some of the myths about pregnancy would be funny were the consequences of them not so tragic. They include such things as:

- A girl can't get pregnant during her period. (False)

- A girl can't get pregnant the first time she has sex. (False)

- If the boy withdraws his penis before ejaculating, you're safe. (Wrong!)

- Saran Wrap can be used as a condom. (Very poor)

- Pouring Coke or Pepsi in your vagina will kill the sperm and prevent pregnancy. (No)

- Taking a quick shower and washing with soap will rinse away the sperm before it has time to work. (Wrong)

- You can't get pregnant if you don't have an orgasm. (Many have)

As I said, even many adults believe these myths. It shows how desperate a need there is for real factual sex education. When it comes to such subjects, don't rely on friends or television. Get real information from adults you trust, health counselors, books, or your local family planning clinic. You need to know the truth.

Reason Two: It Can't Happen to Me

Most of us tend to think bad things happen to other people. We really don't believe that something like teen pregnancy could happen to us. We don't even bother to think about it.

Some teenagers may fear pregnancy when they first begin having sex. If, however, they have sex a few times and nothing happens, they often conclude that they are among the lucky ones who can have sex without any adverse consequences.

Recently, I was told by a counselor at a family health clinic that most of the teenagers coming in for first-time birth control information had been sexually active for nine months to a year. Many had thought they were safe, and only after a year of sexual activity had concluded that it might be wise to take realistic precautions. For some, precautions come too late.

I had a friend in high school who felt it couldn't happen to him. He got tired of using condoms because he claimed they cut down on his pleasure during sex. His girlfriend didn't like diaphragms and was afraid of the pill. So they quit using any means of birth control whatever.

For over a year nothing happened. Their sex life was frequent and quite pleasurable. Then one day I saw Dan sitting listlessly at his desk. Head bowed, shoulders slumped, he looked like he had just lost his best friend. Concerned, I asked him what was wrong.

"I wish I'd never been born," he said softly. "We just found out that Jill's pregnant. What are we going to do? I've got no money, no job—nothing. I just wish I was dead."

Dan and Jill kept their baby. Dan finished high school; Jill did not. Dan found a full-time job and a part-time one as well, to pay for it all. At first, Jill raised the baby at home while she lived with her parents. After Dan graduated, they married and moved into a small apartment.

Both of them are quick to admit that it was not, and is not now, an easy life. They are quick to warn others not to believe the lie that "it can't happen to us." It can.

Reason Three: Contraceptive Failures

Not all pregnancies occur because of lack of information or neglect. Some take place in spite of the use of contraceptives. The plain truth is that no contraceptive works one hundred percent of the time.

Sometimes the failure comes in the use: a girl forgets to take her birth control pills, the diaphragm is inserted wrong, or the condom slips off. Using contraceptives correctly is not as easy or as automatic as some would have you believe.

Others have found that even when used correctly things can still go wrong. Peggy sat in my office and told her story: "I don't know how it happened. I really don't. I was on the pill. I never missed a day and I know I followed the clinic's directions exactly. My doctor doesn't know what could have gone wrong."

Michelle did not want a baby either. She feared the possible side effects of birth control pills, so she used a diaphragm. No matter how inconvenient or uncomfortable, she never had sex without it. Yet, to her complete disbelief and dismay, she became pregnant anyway. Other methods such as rhythm or so called "natural" methods are even less reliable.

From the book *Kids Having Kids*, consider this startling fact. Even if sexually active teens all used reliable methods of birth control every single time they had intercourse, they would still have 500,000 pregnancies, 300,000 births and 200,000 miscarriages or abortions each year!

Without trying to raise false fears, what this means is that birth control or not, sexual activity carries with it the real risk of unplanned pregnancy. This must be faced and considered honestly.

Reason Four: It Will Bring Us Closer

Some teens, and even many adults, figure that a baby may help save a troubled relationship or make the couple grow closer. This really does not work for adults, and it won't work for teens either.

One study of 263 married couples showed they felt babies added significant stress and reduced general marital satisfaction. Those who had strong relationships before the birth of the child tended to bounce back and regain the quality relationship. However, those with troubled or failing relationships tended to become even more dissatisfied with each other after the birth of the child. Far from being a unifying factor, the new baby tended to add to the pressures and, in some cases, helped to end the relationship entirely.

What does this mean to you? Think about it for a moment. If married adults, who supposedly are more mature and better adjusted, find that a baby will not save a troubled relationship, how much more will it fail if tried by teenagers?

Babies should come out of the mutual love and commitment that exists between two mature and equal married partners. They cannot serve to create this love and commitment. That must already exist; otherwise, the whole project is doomed to fail. Besides, using babies as a means to an end is never right. It can only lead to pain and sorrow for all concerned.

Reason Five: My Baby Will Be Someone to Love

When a person feels unwanted or unloved it can be very tempting to try to become pregnant in order to have someone to love and be loved by. Babies are cute and lovable and the deep urge to have one can be a powerful driving force.

Increasing numbers of single women today have openly expressed their desire for motherhood. Often they lack a suitable partner for marriage and the sharing of the responsibilities of parenthood, but they deeply want a child. What they want is to find a suitable partner to physically conceive with and then raise the child alone.

Some teenagers reason this way as well. They may become sexually involved, not because they love or care for the boy, but so they can become pregnant.

Many come from homes where little love is felt or expressed. Some have been physically or emotionally abused. Some may feel completely unloved by family and friends. Under such painful conditions, it's easy to see why a desire to love a small and dependent baby would burn brightly in their hearts.

We have looked at five reasons for teenage pregnancies: (1) sexual ignorance and misinformation, (2) "It can't happen to me," (3) contraceptive failure, (4) desire to save or strengthen a relationship, and (5) desire to love and be loved.

We could have added such causes as a desire to be considered an adult, a desire to rebel and—yes, in some sad cases—rape, to our list. Causes differ and there is no one single cause that can be blamed. What did your list have as the main causes? Could you see any of them happening to you?

I would like you to do something right now. It's really important. Put this book down and go someplace where you can be alone and think about this list and your list and consider where you stand. Come back when you're done.

The Cost

Some teenagers who give birth are happy with their babies and wouldn't change a thing. But a great many are not so fortunate.

Just what is really involved in teenage pregnancies? What are the risks? What are the costs? In this section, we will take a frank look at them. Some may seem important; some may seem of little consequence. But we will look at all of them.

Reputation

In another age the major concerns were, "What will our friends think?" "Everyone will consider us immoral!" "Shame!" "Disgrace!" The basic fear was the loss of reputation. Unwed teenage parents faced social ridicule and even persecution.

Much of that has changed today. Eighteen-year-old Sylvia sat in my office and told me with her head held high, "I did not feel ashamed when I found out I was pregnant and I don't feel ashamed now. I am proud of this baby and want it very much. It really doesn't matter what other people think."

Many teenagers report that the stigma of having a baby is no longer a problem. Indeed, for some it serves almost as a badge of honor: "I am now a real adult. I have something you don't!"

Even so, we can't ignore the fact that it can be tough to tell family and friends about an unplanned pregnancy. How would you feel having to tell your parents? Grandparents? Friends? It can be one of the most difficult speeches you will ever have to give. Social reputation is still a factor with which to reckon.

Potential Health Risks

This can be much more serious. The sad truth is that there may be considerable health risks both to the baby and the mother in teenage pregnancy situations.

Ten percent of all teenage pregnancies end in miscarriage. Teenagers are much more likely than women in their twenties and thirties to give birth to premature babies. Long, painful labor is much more common for teenage mothers, too. In some cases, labor lasts forty hours or more!

A greater percentage of babies born to teenagers have birth defects such as physical deformities or mental retardation. Infant mortality rates are higher in teenage pregnancies. With mothers less than sixteen years old, 6 percent of the babies will die in their first year of life.

Because of the increased risks involved with teenage pregnancies, it is essential that proper medical and emotional care begin as soon as possible. Health risks are real and must not be ignored or minimized.

Social Cost

Teen pregnancy carries a high social cost. The teen years are supposed to be years of growth and development. They should also be years of fun! But an unplanned pregnancy can short-circuit all that.

Shelly was looking forward to her senior year. She would date, go to the prom, and spend time with her friends. She would decide which college she wanted to go to. She could hardly wait.

That summer, however, she found out she was pregnant. For Shelly the senior year did not involve proms, or dates, or gab sessions with friends. Instead, it was changing diapers and 3:00 a.m. feedings and trips to the doctor. It wasn't at all like she had dreamed.

It is hard to imagine just how much time a baby really takes. There is often not time or energy or money for things you may have taken for granted like sports, running around with friends, or for school activities.

Pregnancy will bring you to adult responsibilities very fast. But sometimes being an "adult" before your time isn't much fun.

Career and Educational Costs

Many teenagers who become pregnant drop out of school. This is sad, for many of them will not ever complete their education. Others abandon college or vocational plans and dreams they had for their lives. Many end up on welfare. They may later come to resent their baby for what they perceive as their lost opportunities. This can be terribly difficult for the child and may even lead to child abuse.

Economic Costs

Have you ever seen $100,000? How about $250,000? I haven't either. But do you know that it can cost between 100 and 250 thousand dollars to raise a child from infancy to age 18?

Food alone for a single mother and her baby averages $38.30 a week on a moderate food plan. For working mothers, day care can average $2,500 per year. Clothes, diapers, medical care, not to mention toys and other nonessentials, bring the expenses even higher. Many just can't make it financially. They sink in a sea of bills.

Recent U.S. Census Bureau statistics showed that 73.5 percent of single mothers under the age of 25 with children under six years of age had slipped below the economic poverty line.

Many received little or no economic support from the fathers and were responsible for all household expenses.

Of the fathers who did assume some financial responsibilities, many were holding down two or more jobs. Few were able to do this and continue education or career plans.

Sadly, for most teenagers, pregnancy also means economic hardship and deprivation. The cost in dollars of any pregnancy is high. In teenage pregnancies, it can be simply overwhelming.

Relationship Cost

Many relationships fail under the stress of a teenage pregnancy. Most girls end up keeping their babies and raising them alone. For those who do marry, the national divorce rate is double that of adults.

Many teenage marriages are rocky and troubled. Facing economic and emotional pressures, and lacking the maturity or coping skills to deal with them, can cause many couples to live through a hell on earth. Unfortunately, many times the victims who suffer the worst part of this are the children, many of whom become battered and abused.

• • •

These are some of the possible problems for the teenager who gives birth and keeps her baby.

The alternatives are bearing the child and giving him or her up for adoption, or ending the pregnancy by abortion. These "solutions" also involve risks.

The mother who puts her infant up for adoption will almost certainly experience a painful sense of loss, and perhaps a permanent frustration from knowing that her child is "out there" somewhere.

I'll be straight with you on what I feel about abortion. I believe that to use abortion as a form of contraception is a serious misuse of a procedure that may have a legitimate role in certain situations, such as pregnancy caused by rape or incest, or where there are serious genetic or life-threatening problems.

At any rate, besides the moral dilemma and the possible medical risks, the pregnant girl who chooses abortion can experience a possibly severe postpartum depression, just as if she had actually given birth.

These consequences are real. They are not put here to scare you or upset you. They are here so you can see some of the genuine risks involved in becoming sexually active as a teenager.

If You Are Already Pregnant

To those who are pregnant now, or have already given birth, I am not going to try to tell you what to do.

What I will do is offer some practical suggestions about where you can get real help and support. I also have some words of hope I'd like to share.

First, seek prompt medical attention. Your health and the health of your baby are much too important to leave to chance. It is never too early to begin proper medical care for the sake of both of you. This is a must!

Second, get serious counseling about your options. There are options available to you and you need to know about them in every detail. Family clinics are available in almost every area of the country. A school nurse or teacher can also lead you to proper services. Your pastor, priest, or rabbi, or some other adult you respect and trust, can provided significant support and guidance. Programs are available through such agencies as the Y.W.C.A., the Salvation Army, and the United Way. If all else fails, look through the health pages of your local phone book. There is counseling help available—please use it! Know all your options and what they mean.

Third, don't panic and don't give in to despair. It may seem quite dark right now and you may have no idea where to turn or what to do. You may feel your life is over and, like my friend, wish you had never been born.

Keep calm and seek out wise counsel. Your parents eventually need to be told. You need family support as you sort through your options. Don't try to go it alone.

Though your future may seem dark now, many people have faced this unpleasant situation and have still been able to live full and rewarding lives.

Your plans and dreams may be changed. Some may have to wait. Some may be eliminated. But life is rich and full and, if you keep calm and refuse to give in to despair, yours too can be a good one.

7

There's No Place Like Home?

"**M**y mom is such a bitch!" sixteen-year-old Monica cried to her friend Darlene. "All we do is fight. Sometimes I hate her so much that I can't stand to be around her. I don't think we'll ever get along."

"I know just what you mean," Darlene responded rolling her eyes. "My mom and I don't talk at all. And I know that my friends, Beverly and Crystal, can't wait till they're old enough to move out and get away. I wonder if anybody really gets along with their parents?"

It's a good question and one that many teenagers (and parents) have asked. During your teenage years, it can seem next-to-impossible to have a civil conversation with your parents, much less to be friends with them. While at one time you may have gotten along just great, you may now find it difficult to get through dinner without falling into some sort of argument. It's not fun.

Deep inside, we all want homes like we read about in storybooks or see on television. We dream of being a part of one big family where everyone gets along and lives happily ever after. We want to be friends with our parents and have fun together.

However, what we dream about and what we have are often two different things. We find that we fight with our parents—a lot. It seems there are always new and stricter rules telling us what we can or cannot do. Perhaps our parents fight quite a bit and there is constant tension in the home. Our real-life family doesn't quite measure up to "The Waltons," "Little House on the Prairie," or "The Cosby Show," and we feel cheated.

When I was younger, I often felt this way. My parents had divorced and I envied friends who had "whole families." I lived with my Dad and we really didn't get along all that well. I thought to myself how much happier I would have been if I'd just been born into some other family.

On really down days, I would dream about moving out, but I had no place to go.

Later, things got better and I started to realize that living with Dad wasn't so bad after all. Once I got to see other people's families and the pains they had, I discovered that no family is perfect or problem free.

Getting along with parents can be tough. Indeed, getting along with any family member can be tough because you see each other at your best and at your worst. Sometimes it may seem hopeless. But it can be done. You can get along with your family if you are all willing to work at it.

Why Do We Fight?

There are several reasons why teenagers and parents often find themselves fighting and at odds with one another. I am sure there are more that could be listed, but these are the ones I have encountered most often.

One: Choice of Friends

Many parents clash with their teenagers over their choice of friends. Parents may not approve of the looks, race, or lifestyle of some of your friends. They may fear that your friends are a bad influence on you and will drag you down. Some parents disapprove quietly, while others may openly attack and critize your choice of friends and try to keep them away.

Two: School and Grades

Many teenagers find themselves in conflict over school. Fights over grades, homework, and attendance can get quite loud and bitter. Few families escape them.

Fourteen-year-old Ann was an indifferent student. It wasn't that she didn't have the mental capacity; she just didn't try. Her grades were awful and she was in danger of failing for the year. She often talked about quitting school as soon as she was old enough to do so legally.

As you might expect, her mother was greatly disturbed by this. Threats, pleas, punishments all were tried but to no avail. Not a single day went by that they did not argue about school. The fighting went on for two years until finally, at sixteen, Ann dropped out.

Ann's case was extreme, but most teenagers and their parents end up locking horns over school. Perhaps one reason for this is because school is such a major part of a teenager's life. Parents, deeply concerned that their children receive a sound education, often take it far more seriously than their teenagers do. (Some regrettably go over board, pressuring their children to take the most demanding courses or to make the honor roll each term.)

Because things your parents consider important—like grades, attendance, or course schedule—may not be nearly as important to you, some conflicts are bound to occur. Try to understand where your parents are coming from. They believe that doing well in school can open doors for you. And you know what? They're *right!*

Three: Household Responsibilities

How many times do you find yourself fighting with your parents over doing the dishes or cleaning your room? Have you ever been called lazy, irresponsible, or worse because your room was a pit and your dirty laundry pile threatened to reach the ceiling?

Take heart, for you are not alone! Most teenagers say that conflict with parents over household chores ranks near the top of the list of teenage problems. It almost seems universal.

Shelly's room resembles a disaster area. Her bed is always unmade and her clothes, records, and magazines are scattered over the floor. A half-eaten apple sits on her desk and the trash basket is filled to overflowing. Her room has caused many an argument between Shelly and her mother.

"I can't understand why she's always on my case about my room," Shelly said angrily. "I mean it's my room and it doesn't hurt her at all. All she does is complain: 'Clean your room!' 'Do the laundry!' 'Make your bed!' Why can't she just leave me alone?"

Tina finds that her household chores go far beyond cleaning her room. Last year her parents divorced and Tina's mother is now raising Tina and her little sister, Leah, alone. Many nights Tina's mom does not return from work until well into the evening.

"I have to do most of the cooking," Tina explains. "And because Mom is so tired from work, I end up cleaning and doing laundry and baby-sitting Leah much of the time. I don't mind helping, but Mom doesn't understand I get tired, too. Sometimes we really get into some pretty nasty fights."

Most parents expect their teenagers to assume some of the responsibilities of the home and many of their requests are reasonable. Each member of the family should have areas of responsibility and be expected to carry them out faithfully and well. Don't try to avoid your share of the load. It isn't fare.

Four: Dating

Not surprisingly, the conflict area teenagers mention most concerns dating. Parents and teenagers often differ on the proper time to begin dating, the choice of dating companions, and the activities and schedule of dates themselves.

Cindy was elated. She had just turned fifteen and was eager to begin dating. One hot summer afternoon Paul, an older brother of her best friend, asked her out to a movie and pizza. She accepted immediately and then rushed home to call her friends.

It never dawned on her that her mother might say no. She sorted through her clothes trying to find her prettiest outfit. She planned how she would set her long blond hair. She thought of things she would talk about. Finally feeling prepared, she went downstairs to the kitchen to tell her Mom the good news.

Much to her shock and dismay, her mother did not share her excitement. "I'm sorry, Cindy," her mother said firmly. "Your father and I have told you that you could not begin dating until you were at least sixteen. You knew that, so why are you asking?"

In seconds, Cindy went from somewhere on cloud nine to sinking in the pit of gloom. No amount of tears, threats, pleas, or promises changed her parents' decision. For weeks Cindy felt hurt and angry. It was the most difficult time she had ever faced with her parents.

Parents often fear the new situations that arise when their sons and daughters begin dating. It is something they want for their children, yet are not sure just when. Conflicts like the one Cindy faced are not at all uncommon.

Have you ever fought with your parents over who you are going out with? Do you find your parents are cool to your choice of dates—or even hostile? If so, you are not alone.

Mrs. Prescott could not stand her daughter Julie's boyfriend. Scott was everything she didn't like in a boy. Cocky, loud, and abrasive, he constantly tried to impress people with his macho mannerisms. His dark sunglasses and punk hair style reminded her of people she had seen on M.T.V. She wished he would just go away. But Julie seemed to adore the ground he walked on.

Before each date, there was a battle. Julie knew her mother's feelings about Scott but decided to keep seeing him anyway. While her mother did not actually forbid her to see him, her obvious displeasure and hostility made her position quite clear. Finally, things became so tense at home that Julie and Scott found it necessary to date secretly.

Julie found herself doing things she didn't want to do, sneaking around, lying, and wondering when they would be discovered. She felt guilty and ashamed, yet also angry. "Why can't Mom just accept Scott and be happy for me?" she thought to herself.

As for Mrs. Prescott, her thoughts were more like: "How could my lovely daughter settle for a someone like this? What could she possibly see in him?" She feared that her daughter would be hurt and wanted to protect her. Surely there must be some nice boy she could go out with!

Each side is convinced it is right. Each side believes that it knows what is best. When it comes to dating, parents want to protect their children, while their children want the freedom to decide for themselves. It is not easy to blend this desire to protect and the need to be free. It inevitably makes for some tense times that few families escape.

Many teenagers face conflict over their parents' dating. With the high divorce rate today, over half our teenagers will be raised in single parent families. Many of these parents will date and even remarry.

It can be tough to watch your mom or dad start dating someone new. It can be a shocking experience to discover that parents know about sex, too.

Many teenagers almost assume the role of a parent whose approval is required before any relationship can succeed—or even begin.

Shawn was thirteen when his parents divorced. He remained with his mother, Sandy, who retained legal custody of Shawn and his sister Tracy. For two years, Shawn was the "little man of the house." While he wished his parents had not divorced, he was reasonably happy and seemed to be adjusting well.

The problems began when Sandy started dating an

old friend named Ray. Shawn did not approve of his mother dating and he didn't like Ray at all. He refused to talk to Ray and became moody and uncooperative at home. His grades dropped and he began spending much time alone.

The situation reached a crisis stage on a Friday evening when Ray spent the night with Sandy. Shawn was furious and early the next morning, his fists clenched and his eyes wide with rage, he called Sandy a slut and told Ray to "get the hell out of our house!"

The stress of seeing his mother dating and later becoming sexually active was more than Shawn could cope with. He required counseling from a psychologist, and Sandy and Ray eventually broke off their relationship—largely over the family tension it was causing.

I know from my own experience, coming from a broken home, that it is very difficult to see your parents in a dating situation.

I found that I did not approve of Mom's choice of men and compared them unfavorably to my Dad. I also did not approve of her becoming sexually active with any of them. I resented the time her relationships took and thought she should come back to Dad. If not, I felt she should just be a mother and settle down. Dating and sex were for young people.

It took a long time to work through these feelings. My sister had an even harder time dealing with them.

If you face the situation, it is really important to keep the lines of communication open. Being able to talk to your Mom or Dad about your real feelings is vital. Sometimes it may even require an objective counseling from an outside source. But whatever, remember that parents are people, too. They get lonely and want to be close to someone special, just like you and I do. I know it seems hard to believe, but it's true.

Five: Values, Beliefs, and Expectations

Conflicts over values, beliefs, and expectations rank high on the list of teenage/parent concerns as well. A value is something that is important or has significant worth to us. The problem is that many times what teenagers value and what parents value are not the same. When groups or individuals with greatly differing values are put together—as is the case in a family situation—conflict often arises.

Joyce was quite upset as she talked to her pastor on the telephone. "We can't get our son, Timmy, to go to church any more," she cried. "He used to go every Sunday, but now he just stays in bed. He knows how important it is to us all. What should we do?"

Well, for one thing, Timmy doesn't know how important church is. In this case, something the parents value highly—church attendance—has been rejected by their son who, for the time being, has decided sleep is of more value. That is not solved by a quick lecture.

Such struggles are not at all uncommon in the teenage years. Conflicts over the value of church attendance, school, family time, money, and a whole host of other pressing concerns may seem endless.

Perhaps the most severe conflicts I have observed come over the value of family versus friends and peers. Parents tend to place a high premium on family time and togetherness: things like eating together, family vacations, and family unity.

Teenagers, however, often place a higher value on being with friends and being involved in their own activities. The result is conflict.

Annie's parents were shocked when she announced she didn't want to go camping in the mountains this summer. It was a family tradition. For twelve of her sixteen years she had gone and usually enjoyed it.

"Dianne Gray's family is going to the shore for a month," she explained. "She's asked me to come along. It's not that I don't like the mountains, but this is what I really want to do."

To Annie, going to the shore was a step of independence, a step of growth and identification with her peers. To her parents, it was a rejection of the family and its important traditions.

Both Annie and her parents experienced pain over this clash of values, pain that lasted long after the summer had passed and Annie returned from the shore.

Parents and teenagers who are clashing over beliefs, values, and expectations often report that they can't understand each other at all. "I don't know what's happened to that son of ours!" or "My parents are so strange. How can they think that way?" are common remarks at this stage of life.

When I was in high school my dad and I regularly clashed over beliefs, values, and expectations. My dad did not like long hair; I did. My dad did not like rock music; I loved it and played it as often and as loud as I could. My dad thought school was important; I thought it was a waste. It seemed that we were the true odd couple: we disagreed about everything!

Yet, we really didn't disagree that much. Deep inside we were and are a lot alike. It's just that at that point in my life, our values were different. With time and maturity, many of these things tend to work themselves out.

To be sure, your parents may never like your music, but you may be surprised to find that many of the things they value, like enjoying life and making a meaningful contribution to society, are closer than they seem to the things you value.

Can We Do It?

Can you be on good terms with your parents? Can it really be done or are your teenage years doomed to be times of wars and endless battles?

Well, to be sure, no family is perfect. There will always be some stresses and strains. I love my wife, Karen, very much and we have a good, strong marriage, but there are days when the volume level of our "family discussions" gets pretty loud. So it will be with parents and teenagers.

But you can get along! It is possible to enjoy your parents and like being with them. Problems and conflicts can be resolved, but it does take work. You see, good relationships don't just happen. They are the result of deliberate and concentrated effort. This is true whether we are talking about friendships, dating relationships, or parents. The same principles apply.

Here's some helpful advice others have shared with me and which I heartily recommend. I know these things may sound too simple to ever work, but give them an honest try. You will be pleasantly surprised with the changes they can make in your relationships.

Set Aside Time to Talk—and to Listen!

One of the reasons adults and their teenagers have such a difficult time relating is that they really don't set aside time to talk to each other and to hear each other's views.

Between dating, school activities, part-time jobs, and time for yourself, the teenage life can be quite busy. Including the activities of your parents and trying to make the schedules fit becomes quite a task. Some families see each other only at the dinner table, if then!

Many times parents and teenagers find themselves

dealing with difficult or controversial issues at odd moments or hectic times, rather than when they are calm and collected and have time to consider them fully.

If, for example, you want to talk with your parents about dating and social activities, the time to do it is before you've been asked out and have made your plans. Talk when you are each willing to set aside the time to really deal with the issues at hand.

Alex wanted to get a part-time job. He knew his father was against it, fearing that Alex would not be able to keep up with schoolwork.

Rather than wait until the issue became a crisis, Alex went out to his father's workshop one evening where his father was putting the finishing touches on a cabinet.

As he helped his father paint and stain the walnut shelves, Alex talked about his desire to take a part-time job and why he wished to do so. He asked for his Dad's objections and was able to hear his father's concerns in a calm and nonthreatening manner.

That one conversation did not produce miraculous changes. But later that fall, when Alex found a part-time job he really wanted and was well-suited for, he was able to deal directly with his father's concerns about work and school.

Because the issue had been dealt with before it became a crisis, Alex and his father were able to hear each other. What could have been a major battle was resolved when Alex took the job with the agreement that he would quit if his grades began to slip.

I find that if people are talked to, and heard, they are much more willing to be reasonable and work out a fair compromise on most issues. Problems come when we make demands on people whom we have not consulted before plans were being formed. Take time to communicate.

Turn Down the Volume

You can usually tell who is winning in an argument by how loud each person is speaking. The higher the noise level, the weaker the argument. Noise is a poor substitute for sound logic.

I asked Rachael how she was dealing with conflicts with her mother. I knew they had been fighting quite a lot since Rachael entered high school.

She said they were getting along much better now because they were starting to talk to each other. And more importantly, they were learning to stop shouting at each other.

"Before, when we had a disagreement, Mom would yell. Then I would yell back. Well, before long we would have a horrible fight. Nothing ever was solved," she said. "Now when we have a problem we talk about it calmly. If we start talking too loud, or start getting nasty, we call 'time out' and agree to discuss it when we are both calmer. It really has made a difference."

If you can't discuss things calmly and with a clear head, then it is better to wait until a time when you can. I find in my own life that my wife and I have our worst arguments when we discuss problems when we are both tired or angry. Soon we are yelling at each other and often the original problem is lost in a sea of noise. Nothing is resolved and we both end up frustrated.

If we can sit down and talk to each other calmly without cheap shots or name calling, we usually can resolve most of our conflicts rather quickly and reasonably. Keeping the volume down is a vital part of this whole process.

People tend to copy each other's behavior. When someone shouts at you, what do you do? If someone calls you "stupid," or some other name, don't you feel like responding in the same way? When you talk to your parents, no matter how difficult it may be at times, keep calm and talk to them the way you would want to be talked to. Use courtesy and respect and you may achieve far better results in resolving your conflicts. And it will make your home life far smoother than you could ever imagine. Try it and see.

The Winner and Still Champion!

Many parents and teenagers deal with conflicts as if they were personal battles to be won or lost. They take a hard line, no-compromise position and find it impossible to reconsider without seeming to lose face. In our need to have a "winner," usually everyone winds up losing.

"I don't care what you say," Jeri cried angrily. "Paul and I are going out Friday night and that is final!"

"Like hell you are," her father retorted, "You are staying home Friday and that—you little smart ass—is final!"

Now look what has happened here. Jeri took a hard line position. She announced that she was going out with her boyfriend, Paul, and that it was a final decision, already resolved.

Her father, feeling threatened and challenged, responded with an equally hard line position. He also rendered his own verdict on his daughter's pronouncement by calling her a "smart ass." Both sides felt challenged and were bristling with rage.

They had painted themselves into a corner. By announcing their terms as "final," they left no room for compromise or negotiation. What we have here is a situation where someone must back down, where there will be a clear winner and loser. This is not good and we can be sure that whatever happens Friday night, the real problems will remain.

First, they violated rule one by not talking and listening to each other. Then they violated rule two by shouting at each other and becoming loud and unreasonable.

Finally, locked in combat, they each took positions from which there was no graceful retreat. Each side did just about everything possible to goof it up. What could have been done differently?

The first step would have been to talk to each other before the decision was made concerning the date. By waiting until she had already decided to go and then telling her father, Jeri made a serious error in judgment.

Once the discussion began, both sides failed to keep control of their tempers. Jeri announced, "I don't care what you say," and said it in a smart and arrogant tone of voice. Her father—equally wrong—responded with profanity and name calling. The volume should have been kept down. If necessary, they should have stopped talking until they were both calmer and better able to deal with the problem at hand.

Both sides would have been better off if they had avoided their hard-line positions and left room for graceful negotiation and compromise. Once the issue was moved from something concrete (like a specific night out) to something personal (like parental authority and respect), it became much harder to resolve. Keeping to the issue at hand and not allowing it to become a personal battle to be won or lost makes it possible to leave winning and losing to the athletic field, where it belongs.

Maybe We Need Some Help

Some teenagers are not reasonable or fair in their dealing with their parents. I have often talked with teenagers who are ungrateful and all but impossible to live with. No matter what their parents do, it is never enough. It's sad.

I have also seen teenagers with parents who make life a hell on earth for them, constantly nagging and criticizing, beating and abusing them. They show no love or affection. Some kids have been dealt a mighty poor hand!

I suspect most of you fall in the middle. I doubt that many mean, nasty teenagers are going to read this—or any other—book. And thankfully, the truly rotten parents I have seen are the exception to the rule. I can honestly say most parents love their teenagers dearly and want what is best for them. Try to remember that as you deal with your parents.

Still, there are times when, even though you love each other, things just break down. Sometimes you may find that, no matter how hard you try, communication just doesn't work. Some parents are even unable to get along with their grown sons and daughters.

If you find that communication has broken down between you and your parents, it may be time to seek outside help. Sometimes we are not aware of what is going wrong and causing our difficulties. Talking to an outside person who can help locate the problem can be a big help. It may be your minister or priest or a relative or a counselor at school. Therapists are also available in most communities who will work confidentially with teenagers to help them solve family problems.

Many times, parents and their children can take

family therapy together. You may think your parents would never be willing to, but you may be surprised. Parents want to get along as much as you do. Often, they realize things aren't working out but don't know why. I have often seen parents going for family therapy with their teenagers, especially when the suggestion comes from the teenager.

Getting outside help is not a sign of failure or weakness. Far from it! Recognizing problems and making a genuine commitment to work on them is a sign of great strength and maturity.

Even if your parents refuse to go, and say—as some will—that the problem is with you, go by yourself. In life, we can't control what other people say or do, but we can control ourselves. By talking to someone you trust and feel comfortable with, you can gain greater strength in yourself. You can learn how to better deal with your parents and anyone else. It will be well worth your time and energy and will benefit you richly today and in the years to come.

8

Nasty Secrets

Secrets. They can be a lot of fun and we all like to be a part of them. As a pastor, I have been let in on many happy secrets.

But not all secrets are fun or bring joy. Some are nasty and shameful. Some of the people you know, perhaps even you yourself, may carry the pain of one of the nastiest secrets of all. I'm referring to sexual abuse. It's a national problem and tragedy. For too many, it's a dark secret that haunts them night and day.

If things continue as they are, one in four females and one in seven to one in ten males will be victims of sexual abuse at some time in their lives. It is estimated that there are over one million cases of sexual abuse each year and the numbers are rising. This crime cuts across all barriers of race, age, ethnic background, and culture.

It is not pleasant to write or read about. I am sure for those who are victims, it will be painful to read. But I really believe it is urgent that the "nasty secret" which haunts so many be dragged out into the open and exposed.

What Is Sexual Abuse?

The kinds of things we define as sexual abuse vary. Some children are exposed to unwanted touching. The breasts and/or the penis, vulva, or vagina may be touched or explored by others. For some, the probing is expanded to include actual stimulation of these organs. The child may be forced to masturbate or stimulate the abuser as well.

More involved sexual abuse may include oral sex, known as fellatio or cunnilingus, which involves the mouth and tongue into contact with the genital organs. Ultimately, it may progress to sodomy (anal sex) and in many cases full intercourse.

Roxanne went through all the stages. Her nightmare began when she was ten. One night her stepfather began touching her developing breasts and rubbing her vulva. She found the contact frightening and confusing, but promised not to tell anyone. She hoped it would stop and for a while it did.

Later, however, the fondling and exploration became more involved and frequent. One afternoon, while they were home alone, her stepfather came into her room and forced her to have oral sex with him. This incident left her sickened and disgusted. She begged him to stop and afterward tried to tell her mother. Her stepfather, however, vehemently denied everything and the sexual activity continued, along with threats of physical violence.

Her stepfather, laid off from his job, was at home

much of the time. One morning, while her mother was at work and she was off from school, he took Roxanne to her room and forced her to have full sexual intercourse with him. The experience was so horrible and painful that she passed out. This abuse went on for six more years until she finally got help and was placed in a foster home.

For some teenagers sexual abuse may be long-term, frequent, and involve all levels of sexual activity. For others, it may be short-term and involve lesser degrees of activity. At its worst, it may involve child slavery and prostitution.

What kind of person abuses someone in his or her own family? What signs mark the abuser? Can't we pick them out and send them away before they harm anyone?

The common myth is that people who commit sexual abuse are strangers and easily recognized. We picture greasy old men in trench coats, or scuzzy outlaws who are easy to spot and avoid. We are taught not to talk to strangers and never to take rides from them or go in dark alleys. And we think we are safe.

The fact is that most sexual abuse occurs at home. In 75-90 percent of the cases, the victims are abused by someone they know, often a relative or a close family member.

Sexual abuse may be carried out by a father or stepfather or, far less frequently, by a mother or stepmother. It may be carried out by a brother or sister, grandparent, uncle or aunt or cousin. Blood ties do not stop it from happening.

Others have been sexually abused by adults they knew and trusted: family friends, a minister or other religious leader, teachers, coaches, baby-sitters, or some other adult they would not suspect.

Why Do People Do This?

It is hard to understand why anyone would want to sexually abuse another person. Several reasons are often mentioned.

Emotional Deprivation

Some abusers engage in their practices because they themselves feel emotionally deprived and neglected. Their sexual relationships within the family structure often represent pathetic attempts to establish some kind of genuine physical intimacy with another human being.

Power

For some the need for power is the strongest reason for their abusive behaviors. A father may feel great power in forcing his young daughter to have sex with him. An older brother may use sexual pressure to dominate and control a younger sister.

People who use sex to gain power over another usually view themselves as powerless over most of the people and events in their lives. Feeling so limited, they use sex as a kind of weapon to establish some area of their life where they are "the boss."

Misguided Love

Often the abuser may feel what he or she thinks is love for the victim. One father who had been convicted of raping his daughters apparently honestly believed that his own actions were based on his deep love for them.

He wanted them to experience love in a physical way and was deeply upset that others viewed this as wrong. Even in treatment, he refused to acknowledge any guilt or remorse.

They Were Abused

Some abusers were themselves abused. It's all they know. I always thought that people who had been abused as children would be the last ones ever to abuse their own children. After all, they would know from their own agonies the misery sexual abuse causes and would not want anyone else to suffer it.

But for many people sexual abuse becomes a vicious cycle. It goes many generations back and is passed on like a curse to generations present and yet to come.

Words to the Abused

Perhaps some of you reading this chapter have memories of sexual abuse you endured as a child. Perhaps others have friends or family members who have been abused and who you sincerely want to help. It may even be that you are being abused now.

Recently, I traveled to a nearby city to talk to a juvenile officer whose duties include working with troubled and abused teenagers. He provided me with much helpful information for victims which I want to share with you now. I will present it as simply and clearly as I can and I hope it is of value to you.

The Abuser Is Sick

We need to realize that a child abuser is sick. An abuser is practicing an unnatural and harmful style of relating and must be stopped. Abuse is always wrong and an abuser needs help.

Many victims are afraid to report the abuse they are enduring. They mistakenly feel that they are betraying a loved one or that telling will cause great pain to others. Faced with this, they often choose to suffer in silence.

This is understandable. But it is important to know

that only when the abuser is directly confronted with the harm such behavior causes to all concerned, and with the fact that it is very wrong, can help be found. Few abusers can stop on their own; they need help. Suffering in silence will not solve anything. Indeed, it only serves to prolong the agony of everyone involved.

You Are Not to Blame
Many victims feel they are somehow to blame for the abuse they have suffered. Some abusers have actually accused their victims of leading them on and encouraging the activity. You may find yourself being blamed by other members of your family or friends for allowing it to happen. This can be very confusing and shattering.

But it is never right for someone to violate another person. There is no justification nor excuse. Statements like, "She wanted it" or "He was asking for it, so I gave it to him" are pathetic attempts by the abuser to excuse himself from moral responsibility. Don't be fooled by this.

Some victims feel tremendous guilt because they may have mixed feelings about the experience they have endured. Some have said that they found that in some ways they secretly enjoyed some of the contact at the time. They may not even have known it was wrong. Others have felt great humiliation because they may have responded physically to the experience.

Jane sobbed as she told her counselor about her abuse at the hands of an uncle. The thing that troubled her most was that she had experienced full arousal and sexual climax even though she had not initiated or desired the contact in any way. She felt guilty and ashamed and reasoned that she must be very sick to have had an orgasm while being raped.

This can be greatly perplexing and many victims remain silent because they have found themselves in similar situations. The fact is that the body can often respond to direct physical stimulus involuntarily. The fact that climax or physical response occurs does not mean that the experience was desired or encouraged.

You Must Seek Help

The secret agony of abuse is far too great to bear alone. The strain will break you. It is vital that you tell someone you know and trust about what you are going through. There are numerous social agencies staffed by caring people trained in dealing with the problems you are facing. I have listed some of them at the end of this chapter. Counselors at school, pastors, even the police can also be helpful.

You may feel you are the only one in the world to face the shame of sexual abuse. But you are not alone. Seeking help from people who care can show you how to survive and go on.

Know That It Won't Be Easy

I have to tell you now that if you report being abused, things can get mighty tough.

You may be called a liar or worse. You may experience rejection by your family and friends. The abuser may be removed from the home for treatment. Some homes have broken up entirely after abuse has been revealed. There may be many times when you will doubt the wisdom of your decision to tell.

The cruel fact is that abuse will not just go away. When abuse reaches a point where it becomes recurring and frequent, it becomes almost addictive. Many abusers will not stop. Others cannot, even though they desperately want to.

Your Own Future Is at Stake

You may decide that the risks of reporting are too great and resolve to say nothing. I fully understand this. God only knows how much anguish you've faced already. Who wants to add more?

But by burying everything inside, you will be setting yourself up for very grave problems now and down the road. Many victims of abuse suffer profound psychological and emotional adjustment problems. Left untreated, these can result in serious difficulties in relating to others.

Mary Jo had been sexually abused by her cousin from the time she was eight until she was almost fourteen years of age. She kept the dark secret hidden deep inside and vowed never to reveal her shame to anyone. She was strong. She had survived and she would get through this her way—on her own.

However, though she thought she could bury her secret and move on, she was wrong. She found that she had a great deal of trouble trusting people—especially men. Slim and naturally pretty, she was asked out on dates, but she always refused. The thought of being with a boy terrified her. She felt no sexual desire at all.

Even after she graduated from college she still maintained her deep-seated fear of people. Lonely and depressed, she complained bitterly of feeling isolated and unloved. Twice she tried to commit suicide.

Only after she admitted her profound problems to herself, and went for professional counseling, did she begin to emerge from her personal abyss. After a long and intense struggle, she was—through counseling—able to come to grips with her past and deal with it. Her attempts to keep everything hidden inside had made her miserable and almost destroyed her.

Others have seemed to adjust in a fairly normal way only to discover their serious needs for help later. Filled with regret and self-reproach, they who had once been abused found that they were now abusers.

Physical wounds properly treated will heal even if scars remain. Left untreated they may become infected and can cause further damage and even death. The same can be said for the emotional wounds left by sexual abuse.

There Is Hope

All of this may sound extremely frightening and depressing. You may feel like a mental case, and for something that is not your fault. You may feel doomed to suffer a life of misery and pain. You may fear becoming an abuser yourself.

Fortunately, it does not have to be this way. As I read the life stories of numerous victims of child sexual abuse, I am shocked and appalled by the pain and profound betrayal of trust that has been inflicted upon them. Yet, many of these victims who have had the courage to face their dark, deeply buried secrets, and have valiantly vowed to deal with them, have been able to adjust and be healed.

I pray that you can find the inner courage to search out the help you need. Please don't delay and don't submit to continued abuse and violation. Today is the time to say, "This is wrong and must stop!"

It may seem completely out of the realm of possibility for a young person to do that, but you don't have to face it alone. With help, your nightmare can end. Talk to someone today! My prayers are with you.

Where to Go for Help?

•Some adult you know and trust (teacher, pastor,

school counselor, parent, etc.)

- Your local Child Protection Services (look in your phone book)

- Child Abuse Hotline. Toll Free 1-800-(see phone book)

- Police Departments. Request the officer responsible for juvenile matters. If local police are unable to provide assistance, contact your state police. Ask for the juvenile department.

- Clearing House on National Center on Child Abuse and Neglect Information, P. O. Box 1182, Washington, DC 20013, Telephone (703) 821-2086

- CONTACT or similar crisis counseling help line (see your local phone book)

- National Runaway Switchboard, 1-800-621-4000 or National Runaway, Hotline, 1-800-231-6946

- Your local Y.M.C.A. or Y.W.C.A.

- Your County Mental Health Center

- Your local Rape and Women's Resource Center

9

It Didn't Start Out This Way!

Len Bias was a man at the top of the world. He stood 6'8" and his muscular body, likened by one friend to a Greek god's, weighed 220 pounds. A star basketball player from the University of Maryland, he was the first round draft pick of the world champion Boston Celtics. Bias, in his own words, was "living a dream come true."

On June 18, 1986, Bias decided to celebrate his good fortune by trying some "crack" (a potent form of cocaine) with some college friends. On June 19, 1986, this young man with such a promising future was declared dead by a Maryland physician. Cause of death, cocaine intoxication. The dream had turned into a nightmare.

Don Rogers was a happy man, a key player in the defensive backfield of the N.F.L. Cleveland Browns. He enjoyed all the fame, fortune, and power that comes with being a professional football player.

About to be married, he decided to spend the night before his wedding celebrating with friends at a bachelor party. He tried some cocaine to "brighten things up." Less than a week after the tragic death of Len Bias, Rogers joined him in an early grave; no wedding, no more football, no more life. Cause of death, cocaine intoxication.

Until recently, I thought teenage drug and alcohol abuse was a dead issue that really didn't concern many of today's teenagers. I naively believed it was a problem of the 1960s and 1970s which we had long since solved.

Cases like those of Bias and Rogers began to alert me to the fact that the problem is a real and growing one for all teenagers today.

The Scope of the Problem

In *U.S.A. Today*, the results of a poll of 1,500 high school students from across the nation were released. What is the biggest problem facing teenagers today? According to the poll, the answer is drugs and alcohol, substance abuse. Forty-eight percent stated that marijuana use was a significant problem and twenty-one percent mentioned cocaine use as a major problem of teenagers.

Another article reported that a recent study by the University of Michigan's Institute for Social Research showed that

- 17 percent of 1985 high school graduates had experimented with cocaine.

- 51 percent of the 1985 graduates had tried an illegal drug.

- 45 percent of the males surveyed and 28 percent of the females had five or more alcoholic drinks in a row in the last two weeks.

- Less than 1/3 of the 1,500 students surveyed felt there were any significant dangers or risks involved with trying cocaine.

Mary Bennet French, past president of the Parents League of New York City, stated to a group of parents: "In the next two or three years, 100 percent of your children will be faced with the decision whether or not to try marijuana." The same is true of other drugs.

What about you? Perhaps you have not faced the pressure to use drugs and to drink. If not, I assure you that before long the opportunity will arise. It will be repeated many times over with varying degrees of force and persuasion.

The decisions you make concerning the use of drugs and alcohol will be of critical importance as you live out your teenage years. It is no exaggeration to state that these decisions can literally be matters of life and death, as they were for Bias and Rogers.

Because I do believe that you will face, or are facing now, these pressures and decisions, I have included this chapter in the book. Ultimately you must decide for yourself, but you owe it to yourself to have the facts before you.

Why Do Teenagers Use Drugs?

Why do so many teenagers and young adults feel a need to use drugs? Why is drug and alcohol use soaring to a record level? Must being a teenager and drinking or using drugs go together? What can be done? These are serious questions people all across the land have been asking. They deserve straight answers.

Reasons You Give

Perhaps the best way to learn why today's teenagers use drugs is to let them answer for themselves. These are some of the main reasons given by teenagers for drug and alcohol use. I found them to be quite interesting.

One: Pressure from Peers and Friends

A significant reason is social pressure from peers or friends to drink or use drugs. Many teenagers fear being labeled as "square" or old-fashioned if they abstain. Others don't want to be seen as being afraid. They take drugs in response to a dare from friends or simply to keep friendship going.

Of even greater significance than peers is whether the teen's closest friends are users. Robert L. DuPont, an expert on teen drug use, wrote: "The single main determinant of whether a particular young person uses drugs like marijuana, is whether his best friend uses it or doesn't use it."

Most teenagers, especially in the later years, feel a greater need to identify with their peers than with their parents or family. The pressure to fit in, to join the crowd, is one major reason for drug and alcohol use.

It can be costly to stand alone. For many that is what saying "No" to drugs and alcohol means. For some, the price is greater than they are willing to pay.

Two: Rebellion

For some teenagers, using drugs, getting high or drunk are ways of rebelling against parental authority.

Drug use can serve as a bold statement of independence and rebellion against parents and society in general. Some teenagers use drugs openly to gain the attention and displeasure of others. Often this is a cry for help.

Three: Curiosity

Many teenagers experiment with drugs out of curiosity. "I heard from friends about getting high," Jim said. "I wanted to find out what it was like for myself. It was weird! I don't think I'll try it again."

The wish to find out what it is like to get drunk or high can be intense during the teenage years. In a society which too often glamorizes the use of drugs and alcohol, it is not surprising that many teenagers want to discover this feeling for themselves.

Often linked with this is a mistaken notion that a person can always experiment with drugs or alcohol and then, like Jim, simply decide to quit. For some this may well be true. However, there are thousands of others who become addicted or suffer permanent physical or psychological damage. In some tragic cases, the first use of drugs is also the last.

Four: It's the Grown Up Thing to Do

Many teenagers are users because it makes them feel like adults. Let's face it. Our society really doesn't give teenagers many significant adult things to do. Mostly teenagers are treated like overgrown kids.

Certain rituals of the teenage years have almost become badges of maturity because they are considered so "adult." Obtaining a driver's license, one's first sexual experience, and getting high or drunk have become the big three marks of adulthood for many.

Many teenagers see movie stars, athletes, and even parents drinking and using drugs as a regular part of their "adult" lives. It is no wonder that this is viewed as a part of what being an adult is all about.

Five: Escape from Tension and Anxieties

Phil began drinking heavily as a way of escaping the many tensions in his troubled young life. "Mom and Dad were always fighting. I hated school and I didn't know what I wanted to do with my life. It reached a point where the only time I felt good was when I was loaded."

Though the stresses of the teenage years are considerable, the coping skills to deal with them often are not available. Unable to relieve the pains and anxieties by natural means, many teenagers turn to drugs or alcohol to temporarily deaden the pain of living.

The problem is that taking drugs or using alcohol does not remove our tensions or problems. It can only deaden them for a brief time. After one comes down, the problems still must be faced. No pill, bottle, or needle ever solved life's problems.

Six: It's Fun

A few weeks ago my wife and I were having dinner with John and Diane, a young couple from our parish. Diane shared her own experience with alcohol as a teenager. I thought what she said helped me in trying to understand why people drink.

> I remember going out with my friends and getting totally drunk. But it wasn't because I was tense or sad or rebellious or anything like that. I got drunk because it felt good and it was fun. That's really all there was to it. I guess it's something a person just outgrows.

Her view is shared by many. There are those who drink or use drugs for no other reasons than fun and good feelings. I suspect many teenagers would list this as the main reason. They don't think of it as a problem and really wonder what all the fuss is about.

Seven: Self-Confidence

We often face times when we just are not sure that we have what it takes to make it in life. Haven't you faced those moments when you felt the knot in your stomach, the cold sweat, and the racing heart? We all can remember moments when we had to do something and knew the risks of failing were real and we were afraid.

Most of us get through this. We learn that we can make it. We learn that we can accomplish what we need to and, even if we fail at times, we will survive.

However, some persons never develop a sense of confidence in themselves or their abilities. They are filled with inner turmoil and self-doubt. The only way they can bolster their shaky self-image is by artificial means, like drugs and alcohol.

Some teenagers rely on drinking or drugs to help them get through an exam or an important athletic event. Others use them before some stressful situation like asking someone for a date or giving a speech.

In each instance, the person hopes to find some secret source of courage to overcome the obstacle. Drugs or alcohol are seen as saviors helping them to do what they couldn't do on their own.

Self-confidence can never be found in a substance. There are no magic pills to give it, any more than there is a fountain of youth. People who rely on such means will always be disappointed. In the end, their use of drugs and alcohol leaves them with less confidence in themselves than when they started. True confidence and strength must come from within.

Types of Drugs and Consequences

It may help to know about drugs and alcohol, particularly the potential risks that go with using each one. This list is certainly not exhaustive, but it covers most of the major drugs that you are likely to encounter.

Alcohol

Many people are surprised to see alcohol classified as a drug. Actually it is the most widely used drug in North America today, with users ranging from children in elementary school to senior citizens in nursing homes.

Deaths among teenagers due to drinking and driving have reached record highs. The number of teenage alcoholics has also increased drastically. Many personality disorders and addictive behaviors have been directly traced to an overindulgence in alcohol. Indeed, alcohol consumption has been linked with so many problems of the teenage population that many states are raising the legal drinking age and cracking down on underage liquor sales and consumption.

Alcohol was once thought to be a harmless drug. It is now commonly recognized as one of the most dangerous, mainly because it has so much societal approval.

Marijuana

When I was younger, I can remember attending rock concerts where the smell of "pot" filled the air. At times, I thought everyone in my school was smoking pot except me. Users during my time were found at all levels, from the youngest kids to adults and even some of my teachers.

Of course, there were many who didn't use pot. But the basic view most of us had was that pot was safe, fun, and easy to get. Even some drug experts produced studies claiming pot was relatively harmless. It became the drug of choice for my generation.

Recent studies, however, have shown that pot is neither harmless nor safe. Because of the strength of the smoke, one "joint" is equivalent to smoking many tobacco cigarettes in terms of damage to the body.

Definite links have been traced showing brain damage and personality changes in heavy users. Potential physical effects may include damage to the heart, liver, and reproductive system.

Perhaps the most significant danger is that marijuana has been shown to be a "gateway" drug. That is, many people who start with using marijuana tire of it and move on to harder drugs.

Marijuana gradually loses its power to satisfy and relieve tensions and anxieties. When this occurs, larger and more frequent doses must often be used. Frequently the dosage becomes so large that the person decides to move on to more potent drugs.

Angel Dust (PCP)

Phencyclidine (also known as PCP or "angel dust") is one of the most dangerous drugs in existence today. It comes in liquid, tablet, or powder form and is often used in combination with other drugs.

With low doses, a person may feel a euphoric high with some bodily numbness. As the dosage increases, there may be excitement, confusion, and loss of memory. High doses may result in death.

A public affairs pamphlet, called *Children and Drugs*, by Jules Saltman, covers the dangers of using "angel dust" very well. He writes:

> Violent PCP intoxication can make ordinarily quiet persons into killers of themselves and others. Drownings, burnings, falls, and automobile accidents related

to PCP have brought more death and injuries than any direct damage by the drug itself. Recurring schizophrenic attacks have been seen in treated users. The drug is difficult to counteract or remove from the body and remains present for long periods.

Inhalants

Dale was an adventurer. He always wanted to try new things and was one of the first of our group to drink heavily or smoke pot. He "graduated" to harder drugs and then decided to try a different route than pills or needles. He came upon the "perfect system."

His system was foolproof. He could get high very cheaply with legal, readily available household substances. He could do it in school or anywhere. It left no needle marks or smoke and was very powerful. He was proud of his new plan and used it heavily in the beginning of the ninth grade.

What was his system? Simple: he sniffed glue. Dale used airplane glue and a plain paper lunch bag to produce his highs. At other times he also used deodorants and hair spray. He was constantly high and enjoyed inhaling new substances.

At first his experimenting seemed relatively harmless. He didn't bother anybody and he managed, despite his highs, to hold his own in school.

But by the time he reached eleventh grade, the changes were obvious and alarming. His eyes were red and his nose was swollen and inflamed. He always seemed to be in slow motion with slurred speech and dull, glassy eyes. His favorite statement was a mumbled, "Hey man, what's happening?"

He became a sad joke at school and even other drug users were afraid and avoided him. At the end of that school year, he dropped out—a boy with a blank space where a brain used to be. I never saw him again.

It was sad, but it was also predictable. No drug is foolproof or safe. Eventually, one way or another, a person pays the price.

Stimulants and Sedatives

These types of drugs usually come in pill form and have different purposes. Stimulants ("uppers") are chemically classified as amphetamines. They are designed to excite or speed up the central nervous system. Sedatives ("downers") are chemically classified as barbiturates. Their purpose is to depress the central nervous system and produce feelings of calm and peace. Both can be extremely dangerous when abused.

When I was in college, I can remember some of my peers taking uppers before a major exam or term paper. Some found it necessary to stay awake all night cramming and writing and felt that was the only way they could do it.

Others, who find themselves tense and pressured, resort to downers hoping to calm their nerves and find some peace. Some take such pills in an attempt to cure sleeplessness. Teenagers increasingly are resorting to the use of such medication. They often don't consider them to be drugs.

Many stimulants and sedatives are legal. Some are sold by prescription, others over the counter. The problem is that often illegal street drugs are substituted for those, or the legal ones are abused and become extremely dangerous—even lethal.

Possible side effects of abuse of these drugs include dependency (both physical and psychological), fatigue, depression, convulsions, panic attacks, anxiety, and mental collapse. In extreme intoxication, death may result, often due to heart and circulatory failure. Pretty grim, isn't it?

Cocaine

Cocaine was once a popular and generally considered "safe" drug. Did you know that the original Coca-Cola soft drink was sold as a medicine to cure headaches and depression and contained cocaine until the formula was changed in 1906? Or that the psychoanalyst, Sigmund Freud, thought it could help cure morphine and alcohol addiction? Physicians once used it as an anesthetic.

These examples show how wrong experts and society can be about a drug. We now know that, far from being a safe drug, cocaine is one of the most addictive, deadly drugs in existence.

Today the fastest growing drug problem among our population is cocaine abuse. No longer just an adult drug, it is now regularly used by many high school students and has even been found in junior high and elementary school. One vendor sold it to children from an ice cream truck.

A new form of the drug, called "crack" or "rock," is available in single doses for as little as $10 to $15 a hit. This makes it readily available to all, even the poor.

Unlike cocaine, which can take two to five years to become addictive, crack can become addictive on the very first use. There is no safe or harmless level of usage. One drug expert called it the most addictive drug known to exist.

The physical and psychological effects of crack are terrifying. They can include damage to nostrils, extreme depression, paranoia, agitation and irritation, inability to concentrate and—in the tragic cases of Len Bias and Don Rogers—heart failure resulting in death.

The financial costs are staggering as well. For straight cocaine use the costs can reach hundreds, even thousands, of dollars per day. Even for those using the cheaper more potent "crack," the costs can involve thousands per month.

Because of the high costs, many users, especially teenagers with no jobs or low paying ones, turn to crime and violence to finance their habit. Experts have traced a connection between the growing use of cocaine and rising rates of violent crimes. The social consequences of this drug are enormous and affect us all, whether we use cocaine or not.

Why, with all the proven dangers associated with it, do teenagers still use cocaine? One reason is that they often are not aware of how truly dangerous this drug can be.

Many try it at a party when they are introduced to it by "friends" wanting them to try a new kind of high. They mistakenly think they can play around with the drug and not be harmed.

Others are involved because of the money and power that is associated with the drug. One young man in high school was selling cocaine and making profits of over $30,000 a month! He used profits to purchase a new Mercedes for which he paid in cash.

Others see the drug as the key to good sex. A March 17, 1986, article in *Newsweek* magazine called "Kids and Cocaine" included this quote:

> "Where the coke is, the girls are," says a youthful ex-dealer from L.A. "I had all the girls I wanted. I had all the sex I wanted."

Others see cocaine use as a sign of fast lane, high risk, living. They like the power and mystique that comes with dealing with such a strange and forbidden substance. Even as they are destroying themselves they are unable, and often unwilling, to stop.

Of all the drugs that can wreck your life, this is the worst. No words can adequately describe the ruin that cocaine has caused.

What's Left to Say?

Drugs and alcohol only mess up life. It's not smart, cool, tough, or any other term you want, to use them. Eventually you will discover that you do not use drugs or alcohol; they use you.

Note:

If you have a drug problem, help is available! Two places you can call toll-free are:

*National Federation of Parents
for Drug-Free Youth*
8730 Georgia Avenue, Suite 200
Silver Springs, MD   20910 (1-800-554-Kids)

*National Treatment Referral and
Information Service*
P.O. Box 100
332 Springfield Avenue
Summit, NJ   07901 (1-800-Cocaine)

Also look in your local phone book under Drug and Alcohol Counseling or call your local CONTACT phone center.

10

No Way Out

Brian Miles seemed to have it all. Tall, with deep blue eyes and short, sandy blond hair, the handsome senior was the pride of his loving family and the dream of at least half the girls in school.

"If God was a teenager" joked one of his classmates enviously, "he would look like Brian." But Brian had more than looks. Intelligent and studious, he was a consistent honors student. Largely due to his immense popularity, he had been elected class president. His plans for the future included college, pursuing a degree in law or medicine. For Brian Miles, life was an express elevator to the top.

But Brian would be getting off before the top. One quiet Friday evening, while his parents were out to dinner, Brian slipped into his bedroom, turned on his new stereo, and placing a .38 pistol against his temple, shot himself.

Stunned and grieving beyond description, his family asked the agonizing questions: "Why?" "How could this have happened?" "Why would a young man with everything to live for kill himself?" "Where did we go wrong?"

Shaken and confused, his teachers and friends sorted through tangled memories trying to find some clue to the mystery. What had they missed? What warning signs had been given? Could they have done something—anything—to prevent this tragic loss? It all seemed like a cruel joke or a bad dream.

What did go wrong? Why did a bright and promising young man like Brian Miles find living so unbearable that he decided to check out at seventeen? And why is Brian's story becoming all-too-familiar in cities and towns across the land?

As a pastor, I work with people every day. I had read with sadness about people like Brian, but they were always "out there" somewhere. Teenage suicide involved crazy people in big cities, not decent people in middle-class towns like mine. Secure in my ignorance, I left the problem for the experts to grapple with. Then reality hit.

First, a sixteen-year-old boy in our parish shot himself in the head and, after a daylong search, was found dead in a field behind his home. A twenty-one year old man, deeply distraught over his personal problems, killed himself with a shotgun while sitting at the family picnic table. Three young people, one a close family member and two young girls from my parish, tried overdosing on pills. Only emergency medical treatment saved them from early graves.

Faced with these disturbing and frightening incidents, all happening in a relatively short period of time, I began to fear that the problem was far more widespread than I had originally suspected. My fears were confirmed by the grim statistics. They are not pleasant, but they must be faced.

Numbers and Beyond

Experts tell us that suicide is the second highest killer of young people between the ages of ten and twenty-four, ranking only behind auto accidents. (Many of the "accidents" are probably suicide as well.)

During the hour that it takes to watch a show on television, fifty-seven young people in the United States will try to kill themselves. On an average day, 1,000 young people will attempt suicide and before you go to bed tonight, eighteen young people will have killed themselves. By the end of the year, over 6,500 teens and young adults will have taken their own lives.

Between 1955 and 1975, the suicide rate for the general public increased by just under 20 percent. During that same period, the suicide rate for teenagers increased by a shocking 300 percent—or more than ten times the average of the general population!

Numbers and statistics, however, mean little until we bring it close to home. Look around you. See all those bright faces? The odds are quite good that some of them have attempted suicide, or will attempt it in the future. Some of them will succeed.

Why?

The question we all ask is, Why? What causes young people to kill themselves in ever-increasing numbers? I do not profess to be an expert on suicide, and certainly do not have all the answers, but the following six causes are commonly cited.

One: Low Self-Esteem and High Self-Doubt

People who kill themselves almost always have one thing in common: they don't like themselves very much. They see themselves as failures and are acutely aware of every flaw and fault. No matter how much love is shown them, they are convinced that they are unworthy and not deserving of it. Always, they are waiting for others to discover just how truly rotten they really are.

Along with this, they have enormous doubt about their ability to meet the problems and challenges of life. When life becomes tough, as it does for us all at times, they fear they will not be able to survive the storm.

As children, we tend to see our parents as bigger than life. When we fall and skin our elbow, mommy offers to kiss it and make it better. Dad's, "It will be all right," takes care of a raging thunderstorm or the neighbor's growling dog. We believe there is nothing our parents can't fix or protect us from!

When we become teenagers, however, we learn this is not true. We come to see that though our parents may love us dearly, they cannot protect us from everything or always fix what gets broken. We realize that we must often face the problems and pressures of living alone—and that is scary!

Most teenagers adjust to this and manage to handle the blows of life quite well. They know they have what it takes to survive, and they will.

Unfortunately, some teenagers don't know this. They never felt they could meet life's challenges and are convinced they will collapse when something goes wrong. Their days and nights are filled with dread about things that might happen to them. And when the inevitable problems of life do come, they are unable to deal with them—just as they feared.

When Mr. Madison announced to his family that he had been promoted to the position of regional manager and transferred, they were thrilled. All, that is, except fifteen-year-old Kevin. For Kevin, the news of the transfer and impending family move was about as welcome as a death in the family or nuclear war.

Filled with worry and apprehension about moving to a large city and having to meet new people, Kevin became increasingly depressed and withdrawn. He convinced himself he could never make the necessary adjustments and would always be unhappy. Finally—overwhelmed by doubt, fear, and a feeling of inadequacy—he tried to kill himself by swallowing a bottle of tranquilizers. Only emergency medical treatment saved his young life.

Kevin was one who had been defeated before the battle even began. His biggest foe was not moving or meeting new people; it was himself. He simply did not believe he could do it. Unfortunately, there are many "Kevins" all across our land. They don't need scolding or ridicule. They need help and support so they too can meet and master life's challenges.

Two: The Need to Please

I was lucky. Even though my parents divorced and broke up our home, I always knew that they both loved me very much no matter what. I never had to do anything or be anything to earn their love. My parents would have been proud of me whether I was a janitor or the President of the United States. I didn't have to be perfect, and it's a good thing because I certainly wasn't!

Some teenagers are not so fortunate. They feel they are constantly on trial and must prove themselves worthy of the love and approval of their parents. Deep inside they fear they are never quite good enough and it depresses and discourages them deeply.

"I was always hearing about by brother Rick," Joy said in a quiet voice. "Mom would brag about Rick. Rick this, and Rick that.... Rick had all the looks and brains. Maybe my parents should have just stopped when they had Rick. I'm sure I wouldn't have been missed!"

Bitter and convinced that she was of no value to her family, Joy tried killing herself with a razor blade. Though she survived, the scars—both physical and emotional—will remain with her for years to come.

There are times when pressures are put on teenagers to be perfect. Such things as comparisons to a talented brother or sister, an overemphasis on sports or academic achievement, being pushed to follow in mom's or dad's footsteps, can reduce a teenager to a feeling of utter inadequacy.

There are times when the need for approval and an unhealthy drive for perfection come not from parents but from within. Some teenagers place the pressure on themselves and feel that they cannot love themselves unless they are perfect. They must earn their own love!

If they fail a test or flunk a course; if they strike out at the plate or fumble the ball; if in some way their humanity is exposed, they may become so depressed as to consider killing themselves—almost as a form of self-punishment. We see an increasing number of suicides of this type in our "winning is everything" society. It's tragic and we all must share in the blame.

Three: On the Outside Looking In

I once asked a young girl in my parish why she had tried to take her own life. For a long moment she was silent and then slowly, painfully, the words came.

"Pastor Steve, I don't know if you've ever felt totally alone, but if you ever have, then you might understand. I just felt like everybody had their own life, their own friends, and it was like I was on the outside, looking in. I couldn't stand being alone any more."

It can be devastating to be isolated and alone. Have you ever felt that way? Have you ever felt like you too were on the outside looking in? I sure have, and I remember some others I went to high school with. They were always sitting by themselves at lunch, never going to proms or school activities, sitting alone on the bus, or walking home alone. I wonder if they ever felt like ending it all.

One thing I have found is that even qualities that most people consider good and positive can cause a person to be on the outside looking in.

Matt is brilliant. With an IQ far above normal, his primary interests are science and computers. His bedroom is filled with telescopes, microscopes, computers, and chemistry sets. He plans to become a computer programmer or engineer.

But to his peers, Matt is strange. They want him around when they need help to pass a test or complete their homework. The rest of the time they ignore him. And Matt, alone and empty, wonders if his life will always be so barren and joyless.

Saturday night and Judi is alone again. She thought she had become used to it by now, but it still hurts. Devoutly religious, she sincerely tries to live her faith without being pushy or preachy about it. Because she cannot, in good conscience, participate in most of the activities of her peers, she is often rejected and ignored.

There aren't any young people in her church and, at

seventeen, she has never had a date. Once she worked up the courage to ask a boy she liked to a social event at school, only to be told, "Thanks, but I don't date nuns." The cruel remark left her in tears.

Both Matt and Judi are fine people with truly admirable qualities. Both are loved by their parents and have their active concern and support. And both Matt and Judi have seriously considered suicide.

Four: The Loss Is Too Much to Bear
What is the worst loss you have ever experienced? For some it might be a death in your family or the divorce of your parents. For others of you it may be moving away from friends or breaking up with a boyfriend or girlfriend. Each of us face losses and pains and the teenage years have their share of them and more.

Most people survive the inevitable losses of life and learn to adjust and be happy once again. Even people who have faced devastating setbacks and losses have picked up the pieces and rebuilt their lives. It can be done.

However, sometimes the loss may seem overwhelming. Some teenagers, unable to see any hope, give up. In extreme cases, they decide that life without the person or thing they have lost is simply not worth living.

In Inglewood, California, a young man named Jonathan Moreland stood on his seat during a rock concert and, as the crowd screamed in horror, stabbed himself nine times with a seven-inch hunting knife. He was finally overcome by police officers and rushed to a hospital where he barely survived. His reason for the suicide attempt? According to the police, Moreland had broken up with his girlfriend and said "he could not live without the woman he loves."

The fact is that most teenagers do not kill themselves over the breakup of romantic relationships (if they did, the bodies would fill our streets). Most teenagers do not kill themselves over deaths in the family or divorce or any other loss. Cases like Jonathan Moreland's are, fortunately, extreme and rare.

Five: A Miscalculation

Some suicides happen because of a miscalculation on the part of the attempter. Many suicide attempts are really desperate cries for help with the person really not wanting to die at all. Tragically, sometimes the result goes farther than the person intended.

The tragedy is all too common. We may never know how many teen suicides, which were meant to be cries of help, occur unintentionally. It is sobering to realize that any attempt, however minor it may seem to be, runs the real risk of being final. Such a risk is too serious to take. Someone can help solve our problems, if we ask for help. But no one can help you in the grave.

Six: No Way Out

Some people reach situations in life where things seem so bleak and dark that suicide appears to be the only way out. They despair at the prospect of ever seeing any improvement in their life situations. They reason that death will usher them into a new world where they will be able to find the peace and happiness that has eluded them.

Others see suicide as an escape from an embarrassing or painful situation. Unable to face the consequences of their decisions or actions, they hope for a painless escape by their own hand.

Jill tried to commit suicide after she discovered

she was pregnant. Deeply religious, and the child of devout parents, she felt that death would be better than facing the shame and humiliation of a premarital relationship and pregnancy. This was not true, but in her distorted state of mind it was all she could see.

Mike seriously considered killing himself rather than face the pain of breaking up with his longtime girlfriend. Basically a nice guy who never wanted to hurt anyone, he found more than he could bear the prospect of causing the girl who loved him such pain.

Such stories are quite common, but they do not have to occur. Rarely is there such a thing as "no way out." Even the worst situations when faced honestly, lose their power. Rarely are they as bad as we imagine them to be!

Jill discovered that her suicide attempt had almost been the worst mistake of her life. Her parents were not happy about her pregnancy, but they still loved her and wanted to support her all the way. She only had to give them a chance!

As for Mike, he learned that his girlfriend, while hurt and deeply disappointed, was also strong and understanding. She had known for some time that the relationship had run its course, but had held on, hoping she was wrong. After her initial pain, she adjusted quite well and both went on to rebuild their lives in new relationships.

What Can You Do When Life Caves In?

What can you do at those times when you just don't feel like you can go on? What can you do to help a friend or family member who feels that way? Where can you find help?

Whenever you face dark times and it seems life is not worth living, you need to know that there is real help available to you. Many times it is as close as your telephone.

In almost every area of the country, there are crisis hotlines and suicide prevention centers where trained professionals and volunteers work together to provide round-the-clock, valuable help to those facing crisis situations. You can find them listed in your phone book under sections such as "Suicide," "Crisis," and "Mental Health." One nationwide chain is the CONTACT teleministries centers.

For four years, I served as a phone volunteer for CONTACT and I can assure you that the people involved are caring and committed to what they are doing. CONTACT centers operate seven days a week, 24 hours a day. Your call is strictly confidential and you will find that no matter how grave your situation may be, the people will listen and provide real support during your time of crisis.

If you have a relationship with a minister, priest, rabbi, or other religious professional and feel comfortable with him or her, don't hesitate to call. My wife, Karen, and I are both pastors and we have told the kids in our parish to call us if ever they have problems or face a personal crisis. We have made ourselves available for them at any hour of the day or night. Most of the pastors I have met feel the same way. They are there for you.

Teachers and other trusted adults can be a big help as well. I know many teenagers may not want to call a stranger or a helpline and may feel even less desire to talk to a minister or priest. Where can they go?

For such teenagers, a teacher or coach or some other adult leader may be the answer. Usually such a person is not qualified for, and should not be expected to give, in-depth counseling. They can, however, provide a listening ear and help guide you to where you can get deeper help.

Positive friends are another source of help. (Notice I said positive!) Some "friends" are negative and may be indifferent to your situation or actually even encourage you to take your own life.

Positive friends, on the other hand, are those who genuinely care about you and who like being alive. They can be life savers by listening and providing real support when you need it most.

One friend of ours is going through a time of deep personal misery. He has told us openly of his strong urges to kill himself. Every day is a battle for him just to survive. It's hard to watch and our hearts go out to him.

He knows we care and that he can call us whenever he needs us. Our home is open to him and the guest room is always ready.

There have been times when he has called just to talk. Other times he has stopped by to eat with us and spend time in our home. We have spent many hours talking with this friend and listening to him. It's worth it, and I know if the situation is ever reversed, he would do the same for us. That's what friends are for.

The strength of prayer and a deep personal faith in God cannot be overemphasized. The power of deep faith can sustain one when all else has failed or given way. I have seen this in my own life and in the lives of many others. It works.

I'm Glad I Didn't

Recently, I had a long and interesting talk with a young woman who had survived her suicide attempt. She seemed quite improved in her mental and physical outlook from those dark days a few months earlier. I could hardly believe she was the same person.

I asked her what words of advice she could give to someone who was considering suicide. She smiled and said she could only speak from her own experience, but I think her observations are worth repeating:

> I would tell them never to give up. There is always tomorrow and you never know what good things are just ahead. If you kill yourself, that's the end. But when you hang on, even the worst days can eventually get better. I didn't think they could, but they really did.
>
> I would also tell them not to be afraid to ask for help. My mom and my friends have helped me get through all this. I know now that they really do care. I guess I didn't know that before.
>
> Life is good, even when it hurts. I'm so glad that I didn't die. I can't wait to see what lies ahead. I guess I'm just glad to be alive!

Some Closing Thoughts

In my parish, I have some really special teenagers. The amount of time I can spend with them is limited and I know they all face some really tough problems. I wrote this book in the hope that it would be of real help to them in facing and solving life's challenges.

I also wrote it for those strugglers I have never met—perhaps someone like you. Though you are not a part of my parish, you are still part of a larger family of which we are all a part—the family of God. Let someone in that family know you are hurting. In your own church community are persons who will listen, care, and be with you through difficulties. They can steer you to the help you need and provide a support group to give you courage.

I do care about you and writing this book is my investment in you. Reading it and taking it to heart is your investment in yourself.

I know that no book, however well meaning or prepared, can have the answers for life's problems. Indeed, when it comes to some of the problems we have talked about—like drug abuse, sexual pressure, incest—there are no easy answers.

What I have hoped for in this book is not to answer your problems, but rather to help you to see the powers that are within you to solve your own problems and find your own answers. And I do sincerely believe there is something we all can do.

I once asked one of my young people how I should write to teenagers. I was particularly concerned because I am a pastor. I did not want the book to sound like a sermon preached to a captive congregation or a tract forcing my own religious beliefs on others. Yet I didn't want to deny my faith.

She told me, "Just write the book the way you talk. You don't have to preach or force your views on people. Write your book for anyone whom it might help." I have tried to do that.

However, to be true to myself and my convictions, I must share with you my own source for overcoming the problems of life. This source has never failed me.

I am a Christian and have a deep personal belief in God and Jesus Christ. I find that my relationship with God is the central unifying factor of my life. It enables me to meet the daily challenges of living.

I believe that each one of us, whatever our age or situation in life, needs a genuine relationship with God. The concept of God is an extremely personal one. It is not the task of this book to tell you how or what to believe about God. Others, such as your minister, rabbi, or priest, can help with that.

But I encourage you strongly to make God—however you perceive God—the center of your life. My God is a personal one with whom I talk as a friend. Through God's strength, I can accomplish the task God calls me to. God has filled my life with meaning and purpose and God can do the same for you.

God's love, forgiveness, and power are made real in my life through friendship with other believers. That can happen to you, too. You can find spiritual and emotional support in your faith community.

I also believe that the problems we talked about throughout this book will never be solved until you have a genuine love for yourself and others. People who love themselves and others don't need drugs, promiscuous sex, or the approval of their peers to get through. They have what it takes to make it, because they are strong on the inside.

Because I am loved by God, I love myself. Because I love myself, I am free to love others as well. That is a formula for real living.

You may feel that your life is hard and filled with pain. You may feel life is not fair. Both of these thoughts probably contain a good deal of truth.

I have known some people who have a hard life. In this book, we have seen people facing broken homes, incest, drug addiction, and other pains of living. That can be hard and, God knows, it is not fair. Life is not always fair and never has been! But the question really is not whether we face pains and struggles. We all do. The question is, What will we do with them?

Recently California Supreme Court Justice Rose Bird faced the agony of losing her right breast to cancer and also the constant pressures and criticisms that came with being a judge and public figure. Her words have much to say to us all, whatever our age.

> I'm pretty much a happy-go-lucky person, and I think cancer taught me a lot about life.
> Everyone in life is given a lot of stress. Everyone is given a lot of problems. I think that the answer is not to rail against what is given you, but to understand the way in which you react to it is the real key.

Fortunately, most of you don't have cancer and never will. But all of you have problems, struggles, and trials. Maybe the environment you are in right now is a painful one. Perhaps today things seem at their worst.

Never forget that it doesn't have to stay that way. When I was growing up, I looked at the many things that were sad and going wrong in my life. Some I couldn't do anything about. In life, not many things others do are under our control. But, I also vowed that though I couldn't change the present circumstances, I would work to improve my own future.

When I was young, I used to have wrestling matches with my cousins, Eric and Shawn. We battled for the "wrestling title of the universe." Since I was bigger than my cousins, I could wrestle them both at once. It was always fun, but sometimes it became quite competitive.

Once I applied my famous "brain claw" (something I had seen on TV wrestling) to Eric's head. It was a submission hold and Eric was just about to quit, giving me the "title." Shawn, struggling to pull me off and break my grip on Eric, shouted to his brother, "Don't give up, no matter what the pain!" Eric held out and later, after a titanic struggle, my cousins prevailed and became the new "champions."

It seems like a small incident, and I guess on the scale of human events it doesn't amount to much. Yet I have never forgotten it. Not because of the wrestling "title," but because of the words, "Don't give up no matter what the pain." Those are words I try to live by.

Sometimes the only way to the title is through pain. Sometimes the only thing we can do is patiently endure the pain until we conquer and prevail. If you want to have a better tomorrow, you must first live through today.

A Letter from the Author

*T*o my young friends:

This page is a personal invitation to you. I have a standing policy with my young people that they may call me or ask me questions anytime they need my help or advice.

I make the same offer to you. Anytime you have a problem and want a word of advice, anytime you have pains and sorrows and want to share them with someone, anytime you have a victory or joy you want to share, you can write to me and let me know.

I promise that I will write back personally and promptly. All I ask is that you be as specific as you can and be sure to include your address. You will get a reply. You can count on it.

I hope this book has been of help to you. I hope someday to meet many of you personally. If ever you are in the area, stop by. Until then, I remain your friend through the written word. My prayers are with you.

>God bless you all,

>Steve

Write to me at:
Pastor Stevan Atanasoff
P.O. Box 538
Port Matilda, PA 16870

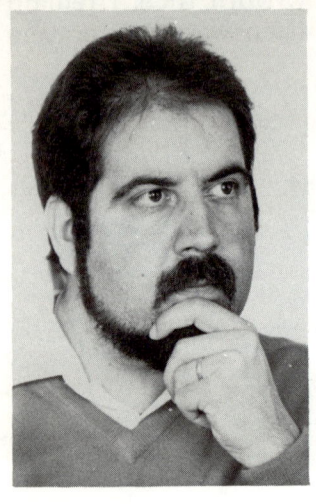

About The Author

Stevan Atanasoff graduated from Messiah College in Grantham, Pennsylvania, with a B.A. degree in Behavioral Science. He holds a Master of Divinity degree from the Lancaster Theological Seminary in Lancaster, Pennsylvania.

An ordained elder in the Central Pennsylvania Conference of the United Methodist Church, he serves as the pastor of the five churches of the Halfmoon Charge near State College.

He and his wife reside in Stormstown with their young son, Andrew Thomas, and their black Labrador, Tyrant.